CROSSROADS

Other Avon Camelot Books by
Paul Pitts

RACING THE SUN
THE SHADOWMAN'S WAY

PAUL PITTS and his wife, Kathleen, lived on the Navajo Indian Reservation in southeastern Utah for fourteen years. They currently live in Salt Lake City, Utah, where Paul works for Jordan School District's Multicultural Program. Besides reading and writing, Paul enjoys visiting schools and young writers' conferences to talk about his books and the writing process.

CROSSROADS

PAUL PITTS

AN AVON  CAMELOT BOOK

"Dreams" from THE DREAM KEEPER AND OTHER POEMS by Langston Hughes copyright 1932 by Alfred A. Knopf, Inc. renewed 1960 by Langston Hughes. Reprinted by permission of the publisher.

CROSSROADS is an original publication of Avon Books. This work has never before appeared in book form.

AVON BOOKS
A division of
The Hearst Corporation
1350 Avenue of the Americas
New York, New York 10019

Copyright © 1994 by Paul Pitts
Published by arrangement with the author
Library of Congress Catalog Card Number: 94-94084
ISBN: 0-380-77606-5
RL: 5.3

First Avon Camelot Printing: September 1994

CAMELOT TRADEMARK REG. U.S. PAT. OFF. AND IN OTHER COUNTRIES, MARCA REGISTRADA, HECHO EN U.S.A.

Printed in the U.S.A.

OPM   10 9 8 7 6 5 4 3 2

For my teammates
and good friends,
Rena Hewitt,
Ilona Pierce,
and
Mongkol Tungmala,
who keep my juggling act
from collapsing.
Without you, there could be no act.

Note to the Reader

Navajo is primarily a spoken language. Although several bilingual schools on the reservation include Navajo language as part of their curriculum and many colleges in the Southwest offer classes on Navajo literacy, the majority of Navajos still do not read or write it. I have included Navajo words and phrases in this book because they would come naturally to the characters in the story. I had to change the spelling of some of those words.

Navajo has a sound called "slashed L." It is made by placing your tongue behind your front teeth and blowing air around the sides of the tongue. The closest English sound to the slashed L is *th*. To make the Navajo words easier to read by people with an English phonetic background, I have changed the slashed L sounds to *th*. For example, a word such as *yíl* will be shown in the book as *yith*.

Navajo frequently has a stopping of breath that is called a "glottal stop." The closest I can come in describing this is the action of catching your breath in surprise. It is a little like a soft hiccup. The glottal stop is shown by a ' in the Navajo word. I have included glottal stops in my modified spelling.

There is a glossary in the back of this book which lists Navajo, Spanish, and other unusual words you'll encounter as you read Hobart's story.

Chapter One

Jumping the last four stairs, I hit the floor, rolled like a paratrooper, and came up running. I sped on through the hotel lobby and into the kitchen. "*Shima,* it's still there."

My mother sighed and started spooning scrambled eggs onto a plate. "Your Uncle Tully will fix it as soon as he finds time."

"*Uncle Tully* is going to fix it? He's no mechanic!"

Holding the empty spoon above the frying pan, my mother had her lost look. "Are you talking about the railing on the top floor?"

I groaned. "The car, Mom. The station wagon parked out in front." I waited for her eyes to open a little wider, a sure sign she understood. They didn't open. "I told you I saw a car right in front of the hotel when I locked the door last night."

"Oh, yes." Eyes wide, she turned back to the stove and nudged some fried potatoes next to the eggs.

It's logical that Mom would think I was talking about the railing on the third floor. We moved here in July, and every morning I'd complained about it being loose. That's at least ninety complaints.

"The people in the car might have been customers, Mom," I went on, "but that stupid sign keeps everybody confused."

Ever since we became the owners of the Enchantment Hotel, the VACANCY sign hasn't worked.

I poured myself a glass of milk. "How are people supposed to know we're open for business?"

"Your Uncle Tully will fix it . . . as soon—"

"As he finds time," I finished and grinned.

Tully Tso isn't really my uncle, he's a distant relative. He helped my mom and me move from Red Rock on the reservation to town this past summer and then he just stayed around.

As a handyman, Uncle Tully's pretty unhandy. The railing on the third floor was a good example. I noticed that it was wobbly the first time I climbed the stairs. Uncle Tully's old, like my grandmother, but he's smart and careful. If he ever "found the time," he'd really be a help. I knew one thing for sure, even if he never started helping, Uncle Tully wouldn't be asked to leave. To Navajos, family is family.

I pointed out to Mom, a guest tumbling down the stairwell and bouncing into the lobby wouldn't be that great for business. But, as she pointed out, business wasn't that great anyway.

"You're the only one who ever goes to the top floor, *Shiyazh,*" she said. "Just be careful."

My mother had taken the manager's room on the main floor and Uncle Tully slept in a little office behind the desk in the lobby. I insisted on having my room far away from everyone else. The first few nights, lying in the dark, trying to figure out what caused each spooky sound, I thought about moving down to the main floor, but now I'm used to the wind and the creaks and snaps of the old hotel.

This place is nothing like the fancy hotels I've seen in magazines. It's just plain and old-fashioned, a lobby,

2

kitchen, bathroom, and bedroom on the main floor, five rooms and a shared bathroom on the second and third floors. Ten rooms to rent, nine if you leave out my room. So far, we'd rented only five rooms and each one was on a different night.

Mom set the plate in front of me and turned back to the stove. I started my don't-waste-a-second eating system by shoveling a forkful of eggs into my mouth. While chewing, I forked up some potatoes. As I finished chewing the potatoes, I took a bite of toast, then a swig of milk. The cycle was repeated quickly and steadily, egg, potatoes, toast, milk, egg : . .

Three minutes later, I leaned back from the table. "Done." I wiped off my milk mustache with the back of my hand and dried my hand on my jeans.

"You're a good cook, *Shima,*" I said, taking my dishes to the sink. She smiled.

"I almost forgot . . . your word quiz."

With a sigh, she looked at the ceiling.

"Come on, Mom, don't hide it. I know you're excited." I made sure she was giving me her complete attention. "The first word is popinjay."

She sighed again.

"Come on . . . just guess. What does *popinjay* mean?"

Shrugging, she said, "Some kind of bird, maybe."

I let out a blaring buzzer sound. "Close, but no points. A popinjay is 'a vain, conceited person.' " I quoted the definition word-for-word.

"Honestly, *Shiyazh,* ever since you found that old dictionary in your closet, you've been driving me crazy." She turned back to the stove. "I'm glad you're interested in words, but I could do without the quiz. I always end up feeling stupid."

"You're not stupid, Mom. You've guessed a lot of the

3

words so far. The quiz is just a good way to help me remember new words."

"Why do you always choose such mean ones?"

I shrugged. "They're the kind that sound interesting." The truth was that, at first, it was just fun to learn words that other people might not know. But since school started, I'd found another reason to look for words ... mean words.

"Just one more. You're doing great!" Another sigh from Mom. I hurried on. "The word is bicuspid. Do you know what that is?"

"It's a tooth," she said triumphantly.

Shoot! What if I was the only person in the world that didn't know that a bicuspid was a tooth?

"See how good you are, *Shima?* One out of two, that's fifty percent."

I rinsed off my plate and set it on the counter. "Sorry to disappoint you, but that's all the words for today. I'm going to go check out that car."

On the way out, I grabbed a small bag of potato chips off the counter and a bottle of apple juice from the refrigerator. The chips and juice were my real breakfast. The other food—eggs, toast, and stuff—that's what I had to eat to please my mother.

"If the driver slept in his car all night," I called over my shoulder, "he'll be ready to rent a room!"

September in northern New Mexico has hot days and cold nights. A few leaves on the tall old trees that lined parts of Main Street and surrounded the oldest buildings in town were just starting to turn from green to yellow.

I stood on the top step and pretended to take a bullet in the stomach. After lurching back against the door, I pitched forward and rolled down the four cement steps to

4

the sidewalk. I'm going to be a stuntman when I get older, and I practice whenever I get the chance.

My dad was a stuntman. Well, not a professional, but he was in a movie once, a Western. He had to act like he was shot and fall off his horse. He did such a good job, they only had to shoot the scene once. Later on, he had to get shot and fall off a cliff into a ravine. He was perfect that time too, except he broke his leg. They didn't have to shoot the scene again either. He was probably glad of that.

This was all a long time ago, before my father and mother got married. I can hardly remember my dad. Working for the railroad, he never was home very much. When I was in third grade, he left for good. I used to ask my mother when he was coming back, but she'd always just shrug and say, *"Haishii yith beehozin?"* Who knows?

The reservation is pretty big and he's from over by The Gap in Arizona while my mom is from Red Rock here in New Mexico. Maybe he visits his mom and dad once in a while, but we haven't heard from him for years. He could be a real stuntman by now. My mom doesn't think so, but it's possible. Maybe he got tired of working for the railroad and went to Hollywood. I used to imagine what it would be like when he came back. How we'd play one-on-one basketball and watch sports on TV together, maybe go hunting. It's getting harder to picture that, but I haven't forgotten him completely. Maybe someday, when I'm all grown up, we'll get together and do stunts in movies. You never know.

I sat up and examined the dusty station wagon parked right in front of me. It was coated with morning frost and, where the sun touched it, small, muddy streams ran down the light-green paint. The insides of the windows were

5

foggy. Someone had slept inside. Probably more than one person; I thought, or a dog the size of Shiprock.

Shiprock is a big landmark around here. Uncle Tully says it's the body of a monster that turned to stone when the Twin Gods killed it. My teacher told me it's the shaft of an old volcano. I like Uncle Tully's story better, even though the teacher's makes more sense.

As I inspected the car, a finger cleared a small circle in the frost on the backseat window.

I scrambled to my feet, turned around, and started examining the front of the hotel. The red bricks were old; their surfaces dull and chalky. What had once been fancy wooden trim around windows and doors was now weathered gray with wisps of ugly, dark green paint clinging halfheartedly every few inches. Mom hadn't turned off the neon sign that hung down the corner of the building. The lights that still worked spelled out CHANTMEN HOT instead of ENCHANTMENT HOTEL. Someday we were going to replace the burned-out letters.

I couldn't keep myself from glancing sideways toward the car. A large, dark eye had replaced the finger at the window. As I pretended to study the warped eaves of the hotel's roof, the eye moved away from the peephole and the door opened.

A girl stepped from the station wagon and leaned gently against the door to close it, as though she didn't want to break the morning's silence.

She was studying me. I watched from the corner of my eye as she combed her fingers through her tangled hair. Then she smiled. "Hi."

I turned quickly, to show that I'd just noticed her. A stuntman has to be an actor too. "Oh, hi."

The girl glanced at the hotel and I noticed the dead VACANCY sign.

"I'm sorry about the sign. Actually, we probably could have found a room for you."

"That's all right. I don't think my dad was looking for a room anyway. We're on a budget."

I nodded sympathetically. When my mother says we're "on a budget," it means we're broke.

The girl kept talking. "We were sailing along to Wyoming . . . well, to be honest, we were *chugging* along, but at least we were moving forward. Then, as we came into town, the car started jerking and coughing. We had to coast down the hill. My dad's going to look at it this morning." She shook her head. "He really doesn't know much about cars. Now, if we had a computer that wasn't working right, he'd know just what to do."

I nodded again, as though I actually understood her burst of conversation.

I walked over and sat on the steps, then opened the chips and held the bag out to her. "Do you want some breakfast?"

The girl hesitated, then walked over and sat next to me. "Just a few."

She took chips from the bag, one at a time, chewing each one carefully. "When we were rolling down the hill in the dark, we couldn't see the burned-out letters on your sign. I thought this place was some kind of Indian nightclub. You know . . . the Chantmen Hot. I didn't want to stop in front. I kept hoping the car would get better and we could at least find a park or something." She stopped with a strange expression on her face. "No offense. I mean I don't really have anything against nightclubs . . . or Indians. I don't actually know very much about either one of them."

I smiled. "You probably thought you were coasting into some kind of creepy bar like in the movies."

"After we stopped, I saw that the sign really said Enchantment Hotel and I felt better."

She methodically finished the chips and I handed her my apple juice.

"Thanks, but I couldn't. I'm fine, really."

I held the bottle in front of her.

"Well, maybe just a sip."

She opened the juice, took a swallow, and tried to hand it back. When I wouldn't take the bottle, she took another swallow. Then another.

"It's so weird—" she rubbed her neck—"and uncomfortable, sleeping in the car. My whole life has been weird lately."

This was the first thing she'd said that I really understood. My own was so ordinary and boring that I wanted to hear more about her weird life. I decided to let her finish drinking my apple juice first.

She blushed when she handed back the empty bottle. "Sorry, I drank it all."

I grinned. "I can get more."

She held out her hand. "I'm Lettie Mendoza."

"Hobart." I shook it. "Hobart Slim."

A high-pitched cry came from the station wagon. "That's Rosie," Lettie explained. "She's three. I'll bet she wet her pants. Mom put a diaper on her last night but she hates to wet one even when it's expected. She's proud of being diaper-free."

My face felt hot and I looked at the sidewalk. This diaper talk was a little too personal for me. "Have you got other brothers and sisters?"

"Just Rosie and me. And my mom and dad. That's plenty when you're living in a station wagon."

Lettie suddenly blushed again and studied a crack in the sidewalk.

8

She looked up when the driver's door opened and a man slid out. In the middle of a stretch, he noticed us on the steps. He smiled and started walking over, then the cry from inside grew louder, and he returned to the door.

"Come on, my little Rosie," he said. Picking her up, he spoke Spanish into the car, then walked around to the hotel steps.

As soon as Rosie saw me, she stopped crying and began inspecting me with her big, dark eyes.

"Julio Mendoza," the man said, extending his hand.

"This is Hobart, Daddy."

I stood up. "Hobart Slim." My hand was getting plenty of exercise this morning.

Mr. Mendoza tried to flatten the hair poking straight out from the side of his head with his right hand while he held Rosie in his left arm. "Is there a gas station close by where we could use the restroom?"

"There's an outhouse behind the boarded up Texaco over there." I pointed across the street with my lips, the Navajo way. "But I wouldn't recommend it. We have a bathroom inside that you're welcome to use."

When her father hesitated, Lettie stood up. "We found the outhouse last night with a flashlight." She shuddered. "If you're sure no one will mind, I vote for using the hotel's bathroom."

Mr. Mendoza grinned. "Thank you very much, Mr. Slim." He turned back to the car.

Chapter Two

By the time I'd gone in to tell my mother about the people in the station wagon, explained that they were going to use the first-floor bathroom, and returned to the front door, the whole Mendoza family was standing in a line on the sidewalk. They looked like steps. Mr. Mendoza was the top, Mrs. Mendoza was shorter than her husband but only a few inches taller than Lettie, and Rosie was the bottom. They all had the same hairstyle.

"This is my mother, Hazel Slim," I said.

Then Mr. Mendoza introduced his family.

"Make yourselves right at home. I'll get some towels, you'd probably like to use the shower," my mother offered. "If you'd like to rest for few hours, we have a room you're welcome to use. This is a slow time for us."

I started to laugh but she shot me a quick frown.

Mr. Mendoza was shaking his head. "You are very generous, but we couldn't. We'll just wash up a little and soon be out of your way."

"How about some breakfast? It would just take a minute to—"

"Again, thank you very much, but we really couldn't. We're on our way to Wyoming. I have a job waiting." Mr. Mendoza was really in a hurry. "I'll just slip in here for a minute and then take a look at the car. I'm sure it's nothing serious."

He went into the bathroom.

"How about the girls?" Mom turned to Mrs. Mendoza. "It will only take a minute to scramble a few eggs."

Lettie's mother shook her head. "We have food in the car. As Julio said, we can't trouble you."

What they didn't know is that visitors are no trouble to Hazel Slim. She lives for visitors.

Mom put her hand on my shoulder. "Keep your eye on the clock, *Shiyazh,* you don't want to be late for school."

"I wish I were going to school," Lettie said. "What grade are you in?"

"Sixth." I leaned close to her. "If you want to, we'll trade. You go to school and I'll go to Wyoming."

She laughed. "I'm in sixth too. At least I will be if we ever get to the ranch."

Her mother frowned at her and shook her head.

"*When* we get to the ranch."

I went upstairs to get my backpack. When I came down, no one was around.

"I'm going, Mom," I called to the kitchen.

Lettie poked her head out the bathroom door. "Bye, Hobart. Thanks."

"Good luck. Too bad you aren't staying around for a while."

"I feel that way too. Maybe we'll be back this way sometime or maybe you'll find yourself in Wyoming. We'll ride horses and herd cows and all that cowboy stuff they do on ranches. I've never actually been to a ranch, but I can just imagine that there are lots of things to do." She wiped away the dribble of water that was sliding down her forehead. "I've always wanted to jump out of a barn window onto a haystack. Do you suppose they still have haystacks, like in the movies? I'll make sure my dad leaves

11

our Wyoming address. When you travel up that way we can get together.''

I glanced at the clock.

''Or maybe we'll be back this way sometime so we can see each other again.''

''I hope so, Lettie. I'll save you some apple juice!''
She laughed.

I went out front and found Lettie's father and Uncle Tully leaning over the engine of the station wagon.

Most Navajos on the reservation are used to getting up early. I was glad I'd kept the habit. It gave me time to do things before school. I leaned over the engine too, even though I had no idea what we were looking for.

Julio Mendoza straightened his back. ''I can't see anything out of place. Is there a garage in town . . . a tow truck?''

Uncle Tully straightened up too. ''There's a mechanic at the Sinclair, no tow truck. Used to be. Broke down.''

Mr. Mendoza laughed. ''Just my luck.''

Uncle Tully went on. ''I got a pickup. We can pull this *chidi* to the Sinclair.''

I wanted to help them tow the station wagon, but my mother has definite ideas about education. One reason we'd moved to town was so that bad roads wouldn't keep me from getting to school. With a sigh, I shouldered my backpack and headed down the street.

It wouldn't make Lettie's dad happy, but I'd be glad if the mechanic had to order a part. That way the Mendozas would be here until afternoon. At least we'd have company for lunch, my mother would see to that.

Most days, I was one of the first kids to get to school. I liked to pick out a place to wait for the bell to ring. Sometimes Lorenzo Manygoats showed up and wandered

12

over to stand by me. He never said much, but if standing by someone is an act of friendship, I guess you could call us friends. At least Lorenzo was the closest thing to a friend that I had so far.

As usual, the crowd had gathered under the big tree in front of the school just before the bell. Calvin Benally was at the center of the crowd. Every time he noticed me, he had something to say.

"Kind of late today, aren't you, Ho-o-o-bar-r-rt?" He stretched my name out, making it sound like a joke. "Did you have trouble getting dressed? I guess it's hard to get your pants to stay up when you're so *slim*."

Some of the kids laughed, but a lot of them just looked at the ground, relieved that I was getting Calvin's treatment and not them.

"Couldn't even find time to comb your hair or brush your teeth, could you?" Calvin said. He turned to his audience. "Maybe they don't know about stuff like that out on the *rez*."

As usual, I had my response all planned out, like a scene in a movie. I flashed him my biggest grin. "Thank you, Calvin."

He looked at me suspiciously.

"I hope you know how much we all appreciate you. Most people wouldn't go out of their way to improve things. But you always take time to give me pointers on how to make myself better. Doing friendly stuff like that seems to be easy for you."

As I moved closer to him, Calvin clenched his hands into tight fists. I kept talking. "I know I'll never be a genuine *popinjay* like you, Calvin, but I'm doing my best."

Calvin looked at the other kids but, as usual, they were just as confused as he was.

13

"The important thing is, with your encouragement, I'm going to keep working until my *bicuspids* are as big as yours." I gave his upper arm a squeeze. He just stared at me.

I walked away, leaving Calvin Benally flexing what he thought were his bicuspids. "That guy is crazy," I heard him mumble to his friends.

So far, I hadn't been able to figure it out. I'd never done anything to make him mad, but Calvin, a Navajo like me, just seemed to have something against people who came from out on the reservation.

During the summer, right after we'd moved in, I thought he was picking on me because I was new in town. Surely the teasing would stop after he got to know me better. But we'd been in school almost a month and Calvin hadn't let up.

I guess every school has a Calvin Benally in it. Nobody really seemed to like him but they went out of their way to stay on his good side. Getting teased made me mad, but my real worry was I didn't have any friends. As long as I was Calvin's target, none of the other kids would take the chance of becoming friendly. Ridiculing him without letting him in on the joke was just a way to make up for letting Calvin push me around instead of knocking his block off.

Thank goodness for Lorenzo. He hung around me whether Calvin liked it or not. With a last name like Many-goats, maybe he had been Calvin's last victim.

As usual, as soon as Calvin's back was turned, I gave him what I hoped was a dark, mean stare and kept walking. The truth was, I didn't know Calvin well enough to figure out how to really insult him. What could possibly bother a rotten kid like him? What I really wanted to do was jump on him, knock him to the ground, sit on his chest, and pound his face. Pound my fists against it again and again, until it was mush. I would never actually do something like that. I'm a pacifist. That means I don't believe in fighting.

I don't believe in putting myself in danger either. Every time I thought about smacking him, I'd think about Calvin hitting back, about Franklin or Leo or Raymond joining the fight. Stuntmen have to be tough, but there's no use taking risks when the cameras aren't rolling.

"Uh . . . Hobart?" It was Lorenzo Manygoats.

I looked over at him.

"Um . . . a bicuspid is a tooth."

I smiled. "I know."

Lorenzo smiled back, then his face grew serious. "It's in the health book . . . *bicuspid,* I mean. We're going to get to that chapter one of these days."

I shrugged. "Maybe Calvin will be absent that day . . . or forget that I said he had big bicuspids by the time we study teeth."

Lorenzo smiled again. "I hope so."

"Thanks."

I was too far away to hear what Calvin said but some kids laughed. It made me feel lonesome, a little homesick for Red Rock and my cousins and old friends.

Maybe Lettie would have to stick around. Maybe she'd come to school and take my place as the new kid. At first, the thought gave me a rush of hope. Then shame slid in and I felt like a creep. I wouldn't want that misery for anybody, especially a nice person like Lettie Mendoza.

15

Chapter Three

The black minute hand on the clock above the chalk-board wasn't moving. From the corner of my eye, I could see the second hand creeping past each number, but the minute hand seemed stuck between two and three. Eleven-thirteen. Lunch was never going to get here!

I watched Calvin flex his "bicuspid," then start drawing again on the back of his notebook. The picture was sort of a mutant-type human. He drew a knife sticking out of the ear and arrows piercing the top of the head like a crown. When he scribbled tight curls all over the head I knew it was supposed to be Mrs. Buckley. Calvin drew her picture almost every day. In every portrait she was suffering some form of terrible torture.

Everyone was bored. Eleanor Jelly was giving her book report, telling every single thing that happened in the book. She would have saved time if she'd read the whole book to us. "Remember, class," Mrs. Buckley had said a thousand times, "a book report should *summarize* the main events of the book and make other people want to read it for themselves." I guess Eleanor didn't understand. Now, there wasn't a single person in our class who would come within a hundred feet of that book.

I tapped my fingers together, trying different rhythm patterns to match the music floating down the hall from another classroom. This reading stuff was using up important math time, and math's my favorite subject. On last year's report card, Mr. Toledo wrote, "Hobart is fast and accurate at computation." I was hoping for the same sort of praise from Mrs. Buckley. But we were already way into math time. I glanced up at the clock again and sighed.

At eleven-thirty-six, Eleanor asked, "Does anyone have any questions?"

I thought about asking one just to see everybody faint, but before I could, Mrs. Buckley jumped in. "Thank you, Eleanor. Remember, class, you don't need to tell the whole story, just summarize the important parts of the book." She was rubbing the sleep from her eyes. Then she walked over to her desk and picked up her math book. "Will you please take out your arithmetic homework?

"Pass your paper to the person behind you. The last person in the row, bring your paper to the front."

Sometimes we passed our papers to one side or the other or to the person in front, but we never corrected our own. Mrs. Buckley worried about cheating.

I watched Calvin pass his paper to Daisy and hold up two fingers. Daisy nodded.

For the next few minutes, the teacher sat at her desk and read the answers. If she had walked around the room, she might have seen Daisy furiously correcting wrong answers. She didn't walk and she didn't catch the cheating. She never did.

"As I call the name of the person whose paper you corrected, give me the total number of problems he or she missed," Mrs. Buckley said, opening her grading notebook.

When she got to Calvin Benally, I thought, *Two,* just as Daisy called out, "Two." I couldn't figure out what

Calvin did on real tests, the kind the teacher corrects. Knowing Calvin, he had found a way to beat the system.

When Mrs. Buckley called, "Hobart?" I thought, *Zero*, just as Lorenzo said the score. Yes! I'd double-checked every answer last night.

There was just enough time for Mrs. Buckley to give us a homework assignment. "Page thirty-three. Problems one through thirty. Multiplication by three digits."

The class groaned. Not me, I love math. If I hadn't been so anxious to find out what was going on with the Mendoza family, I'd have stayed a few minutes into the lunch hour to work the first few problems.

Instead, I slammed my book and threw it into the desk before the bell finished ringing. Its echo was still bouncing around the hall as I ran out the front door. I was in such a hurry, I didn't even take the time to get ambushed by the big tree in front of the school. Practicing for my stunt-man career would have to wait.

As I rounded the corner, I noticed that the green station wagon was gone. Uncle Tully was squirting water into the lilac bushes in the shady sideyard. Watering was one thing he found the time to do, and the tall trees, grass, and shrubs at the side and back of the old hotel had flourished since we'd moved in.

I stopped running and gave a disappointed sigh. Shoot, just my mother, Uncle Tully, and me for lunch . . . boring. Suddenly the bright white of Rosie Mendoza's clothes flashed into view as she walked from behind a tree to help Uncle Tully hold the hose. All right! Company was worth a burst of energy. I started running again.

As I reached the corner, Lettie slipped out the door and waved.

"Were you waiting for me?" I panted for a few seconds to catch my breath.

"All morning. What did you do at school?"

I shrugged. "Same old stuff, reading, English, math . . ."

"Sounds fun, except for the math." She grabbed my shoulder to keep me on the porch. "My dad let me go to the gas station with him and your uncle and I heard everything the mechanic said. The car is a mess. It might take a couple of weeks to fix it, maybe even a month. And they have to order parts. Even if they get it fixed fast, my dad doesn't have much money to pay for it. He's afraid he'll lose the job in Wyoming if he doesn't show up on time. Your mom told him that she thinks the guy at the station will let him make payments over time but if she thinks he'll go for that, she doesn't know my dad."

That girl could really talk! I had exactly the same feeling I'd had when the toilet on the third floor overflowed. Like water slopping over the bowl and splashing onto the old linoleum, Lettie's words just kept coming in an overwhelming rush. I tried to think of something to say, but it didn't matter. She didn't pause for a second. The sound of her chatter, like the gurgle of a neverending flush, kept washing over me.

"Your mom tried to get my dad to call the ranch and explain the situation but he's too proud. He doesn't want them to hold the job for him because they feel sorry for him. He's such a dope!" She shook her head and grinned. "I don't mean he's really a dope, he's just too proud. Your mother tried to give us some breakfast, but my dad said, No way, so we had to eat donuts and milk for breakfast. The milk wasn't even very cold. Except I already ate your chips and juice so I was better off than the others. And we'll have to eat that same thing for lunch, except the milk is cold now 'cause your mom insisted on putting it in the refrigerator. You're having this stuff that smells wonderful for lunch, wrapped in tortillas—"

I held up my hands. "Stop! I give up. I'll sneak you some hash and tortillas."

Lettie looked surprised, then embarrassed. "No way, Hobart. We Mendozas don't accept charity."

I laughed. "It isn't charity, it's friendship. All that other stuff will work out too. As soon as my mother thinks up some good ideas, she'll talk your dad and mom into doing something sensible about the problem. She's a very practical person."

Like Lettie said he would, her father insisted on feeding his family himself. After lunch, with a few minutes before school started again, I sat with Lettie on the back porch.

"Is your name really Lettie?"

She nodded. "It's short for Leticia."

"That's pretty. Maybe I'll use your full name. No offense, but Lettie sounds . . . strange."

She laughed. "I can't believe a kid named Hobart is telling me my name is strange."

It was my turn to laugh. "I guess Hobart is a little unusual."

"Is it a family name?"

"In a way . . . My grandmother worked in the kitchen at a boarding school when she was young. Every day she loaded dirty lunch trays into a dishwasher that had a shiny metal nameplate on the side: Hobart. I guess it's the most beautiful English word she ever saw." I noticed my loose shoelace and started tying it. "So, when I was born, she talked my mother into naming me Hobart."

Lettie smiled. It was a friendly smile, not a smirk. "I like a name with a story behind it."

"It could have been worse." I grinned. "I could have been named Maytag or General Electric."

Lettie laughed.

Even though I didn't want to, I stood up. "I'd better

get back to school. Don't worry about things, Leticia . . . the car and the job and all that other stuff. I'm serious when I tell you my mother is pretty smart. She's also persistent. She'll talk your dad into doing the right thing. He'll give in by suppertime." I started down the steps. "He can't escape from her without a car!"

She laughed again, and all the way back to school I was glad I'd made her laugh.

When I found Lorenzo Manygoats waiting for me just inside the main door, I wasn't surprised. Lots of times in the last three weeks, I'd looked around and found him standing next to me. The surprise was that he actually spoke to me again. Twice in one day was a record.

"I was wondering . . . if you have some free time after school . . . maybe we could find something to do . . . together."

"Well . . . sure . . . I'd like that," I stammered, then I remembered Lettie. "The only thing is we have these people staying at the hotel . . . guests. I may have to do something with them . . . to help, you know."

Lorenzo nodded. "Maybe another time."

"Why don't you just come over? That'll be okay."

Lorenzo shook his head and turned toward the classroom. "That's okay. I don't want to get in the way. Maybe we can do something when those people are gone . . . unless some new ones show up."

All afternoon, I kicked myself for being a dope. Lorenzo's invitation had been the first step toward friendship that anyone had made and I'd turned him down. I decided to get Lorenzo to come over anyway. Three of us thinking of things to do would be better than two. I'd talk to Lorenzo right after school.

Unfortunately, when I stood on the top step, searching

21

the crowded schoolyard for him after the last bell, I couldn't spot Lorenzo anywhere.

On the way up to my room to change my clothes, an evil gangster hit me over the head with a board just as I reached the landing on the second floor. I fell forward, against the wall, then waited long enough for him to think I was finished off. Step by step, I pulled myself up toward the top floor. As usual, I didn't get near the railing on the staircase. It was a habit now. When we first moved in, I'd forget and try to use it to help pull myself up. The banister would shudder crazily, and all sorts of pictures would spring into my head with me dropping ungracefully down to the lobby. When I'd get downstairs after scaring myself, I'd complain about it and Uncle Tully would slowly climb the stairs. He'd shake the creaking banister for a few seconds and mumble, "Not so bad, *Shida'*." Then I'd follow him slowly down the stairs as he promised, "I can fix it as soon as I find time."

After a quick change into old clothes, I stepped into the hall and almost passed out. Leticia Mendoza was holding her little sister up to the railing so Rosie could peer down to the floors below.

My stuntman's instincts took over. No matter how dangerous it was, I had to keep my thoughts calm. I crept slowly, silently behind them. With one lightning-fast, heroic motion, I grabbed them both in a bear hug that brought stereophonic screams, and pulled them back to the wall.

"What are you doing?" Lettie elbowed herself free.

Scrambling to my feet, I picked up Rosie, who was quickly following her original scream with a whimper. Holding her and patting her back, I was suddenly homesick for Red Rock. For my little cousins. I looked over at Lettie.

"I was probably saving your life," I said in a cool hero's voice. "I'm surprised you didn't notice it yourself, little lady. That railing is ready to crash down any minute!"

"What do you mean, 'little lady'? Hobart, you're so strange." She walked over and shook the banister. It didn't even move.

With my mouth hanging open, I tried to wiggle it. It was solid!

"My dad fixed it," Lettie explained. "He had to call the Flying Deuce Ranch, but he wouldn't use the phone until your mother gave him a way to earn the call." She pounded the railing again. "He's not very handy with cars but he's good with buildings."

"I'll say." I grabbed the wood one more time. Then I shifted Rosie to my other hip and she pounded the banister a couple of times and smiled.

"It's not easy, having your life saved, is it, Rosie Mendozie?" I said, and her dark eyes sent one more stab of homesickness through me. Then I carried her down the stairs.

We found her mother sitting on one of the old sofas in the lobby, leafing through magazines. As the baby crawled into her lap, my mom came in.

"I just made some iced tea, Cecelia. Come taste it for me."

With a smile, Mrs. Mendoza nodded and followed her into the kitchen, Rosie still in her arms.

"So, what's the latest news?" I asked.

"News?"

"Come on, Lettie, are you guys staying around for a while or not? At lunch you couldn't stop talking!"

23

Lettie grinned. "If you promise not to call me 'little lady' anymore, I'll tell you what I know."

"It's a deal." I held out my hand and she shook it.

She checked to see that her mother was still in the kitchen. "Actually, I don't know anything. Every time I walk into a room when my parents are talking, they stop and wait for me to leave."

I'd had that experience with grown-ups myself. In a few seconds, I motioned her over with my finger. "I've got an idea. Come on." I headed for the stairs and Lettie followed.

On the third floor, I stopped at a door next to the bathroom. "The best thing about old buildings is that they're full of surprises."

Slowly, as quietly as I could, considering its pioneer hinges, I opened the door. "These stairs go down to the kitchen. I think cooks and maids used them to get from their rooms up here to the main floor without disturbing the guests."

"Did you make that up?"

I blushed. "Yes, but it makes sense, doesn't it?"

She gave me a skeptical smile.

I stepped into the passageway. "The boards are creaky so walk next to the wall."

Like snails we eased our way down. Each time a stair squeaked, we'd stop and wait a few seconds. From the second floor to the kitchen, we moved like we were pulling ourselves through yesterday's oatmeal. Luckily Rosie, playing with pans and lids on the floor, covered a lot of the creaks and snaps. We settled down right behind the kitchen door, the perfect position for eavesdropping.

After five long minutes, I gave up hope of hearing anything important. Our mothers seemed to be stuck on the subject of tea: green, black, herb, Navajo tea, iced, hot . . .

24

Pulling on my sleeve, Lettie pointed upstairs, but I held up my hand. There was a lull in the conversation, and a creaky stair right then would give us away for sure.

"You know, I wish that husband of yours would let us help him work things out," my mom said.

There was a soft sputter from Lettie's mother, a tiny half-laugh. Then a long silence. "Julio is a very fine man. I should tell you something about him . . . about us, so you will understand." There was another pause. Maybe she was checking to see that Lettie's dad wasn't around. "He wouldn't like for me to share this with just anyone, but you have been very kind."

We heard her sip her iced tea. "He is stubborn and proud, but sometimes those are good qualities. He's also very smart. He was a manager with an electronics company, a fine job, a growing industry. And everyone liked him, respected him."

Another sip of tea. "The company grew too fast, found themselves in financial trouble and had to cut back. Julio was pushed into the position of thousands of people in this country, he was without a job. But he was proud and stubborn and smart.

"We had some savings and he began immediately, that very night, to apply for a new job. He refused to believe that he wouldn't find one. But every company was becoming cautious, cutting back or at least not hiring new people. No matter how good my Julio was, no one could find a place for him."

Rosie began to fuss. "Here, *at'eed yazhi,*" Mom said. "Have a cookie. One won't spoil your appetite for supper."

Lettie's mother continued. "He took a job managing a movie house but the wage was low. We had to trade in our cars for the antique station wagon that now sits at the gas station. Then we sold our house, making hardly any profit, and our savings kept shrinking.''

We could hear her sigh. ''Now I will tell you how my husband is different from many who have lost their jobs. He would not get discouraged and he wouldn't wait until we had lost everything, until we had to go on welfare. He worked out a plan to keep us from becoming *hope*less . . . even though we were *home*less.

''As a teenager, Julio worked two summers on a ranch in Colorado. He loved it. It's been his dream to return to that life. He's not a real cowboy, but he loves the country, the fresh air. So he gathered names and addresses of large ranches, sent them a letter explaining how a computer system could help their business and why he was the man to set up such a system. He heard from many saying they couldn't afford such a luxury. A few called to find out more about his ideas. And one, the Flying Deuce, paid for his airline ticket to Wyoming so they could meet him face to face and find out more about his computer system. Not long after that, they offered him a job. We almost made it to the dream ranch.''

My mother spoke up. ''When he called them this afternoon, why didn't he just explain the situation? I'm sure they'd help you get to Wyoming.''

''After taking care of us so well, after working so hard, it's difficult for Julio to ask for help.'' Her voice moved to the sink. The faucet was turned on. ''He has given the Flying Deuce the idea that he's a successful businessman, not a man who's desperate for a job. He doesn't want to change that image. It may not make sense to us, but it is his way.''

''What did he tell them when he called today?''

''Only that he has some business to take care of that's taking longer than he thought. They told him he doesn't

26

need to hurry. They will hold the job until January or February if he wants. That gives him time to get the computer system in place before their busy season starts.''

I heard my mother open the cupboard under the sink. Then a thud on the counter, a bag of potatoes. "Then all we have to do is work out a way to pay for the car repairs and convince him to stay on here at the Enchantment Hotel until you're on your feet again."

"A big challenge," Mrs. Mendoza said with her funny laugh.

"We can do it, Cecelia." Mom opened a drawer, then turned on the faucet. "Right now, the challenge is dinner. I've got to cut some potatoes into this stew. One way or another, your family is going to eat with us tonight."

"It smells wonderful."

"Thanks." Mom's voice moved to the back door. "One other challenge at the moment is getting Hobart to do his jobs. If I don't remind him, he'll be doing them in the dark again."

Lettie and I looked at each other and winced.

"Shiyazh!" Mom called out the door and waited. In a minute, we could hear her calling from the lobby. Luckily, Lettie's mom said, "Come on, Rosie." We heard her moving into the hall.

We waited a few seconds, then slipped into the kitchen and out the back door. Racing around to the front, we arrived winded at the hotel entrance.

"Were you calling?" I panted.

"The trash cans," Mom said.

"I was just going to do them."

"I'll help," Lettie volunteered.

Chapter Four

My most important job on the Hazel Slim Slavery List was picking up litter from around the hotel and emptying all the trash cans into the big bin in back. According to Mom, the most important trash cans to keep empty were the "Keep America Beautiful" cans that sat on the sidewalk in front of the building.

"Those cans make a first impression on our guests," she said when we first moved in.

"What guests?" I whispered to myself. The mystery to me was how stuff even got in them, since nobody seemed to drop by to get that first impression.

While I was picking up stray papers from around the steps, Lettie disappeared. Smart girl, I thought. But she returned in a few seconds with a broom from the back porch and started sweeping the sidewalk.

"What are you doing?"

"Just cleaning up a little."

"You don't have to do that."

"I know. I like to keep busy. Even when I was a little girl, if my dad was cleaning the garage or something, I'd start sweeping. I didn't stop when the garage was done, I'd keep sweeping and do the driveway and the sidewalk. Just to stay busy."

Never sure how long a conversation with Leticia would

28

last, I decided I'd better get busy myself. I emptied the cans at each corner of the hotel into the one by the front door and took it around back.

I was just coming out of the alley with the trash can when I noticed a bike heading down Main Street. Sunlight flashed off the rider's dark glasses. It was Calvin Benally. Since I didn't feel like being insulted in front of Lettie Mendoza, I ducked back around the corner. I didn't run or anything, just settled myself into an inconspicuous spot.

Calvin noticed Lettie sweeping the sidewalk and slammed on his brakes, sliding a few yards across the pavement. Then he continued down the block, turned around, and came back. He cruised on up the street twenty yards, then circled sharply, his foot gliding on the pavement to steady the turn, then back down the street he sped. This time, as he pedaled past, he clasped his hands behind his head, turning to keep his gaze on Lettie.

Shoot, Calvin was actually showing off for her! What was worse, Leticia seemed to be enjoying the show! I forgot all about staying inconspicuous and started around the corner. With all his attention focused on impressing Lettie, Calvin didn't even notice me.

He also didn't notice that his bike was angling off toward the alley next to the hotel or that I was standing there with a "Keep America Beautiful" trash can in my arms.

I yelled, "Look out!" in plenty of time for him to correct his course. If I'd known his reflexes were so slow I would have yelled earlier. He seemed to wake up just as his front tire grazed the trash can, knocking it out of my arms. It clattered across the alley.

"Watch where you're going!" Calvin said. Then, shooting an embarrassed glance at Lettie, he sped on down the street.

Lettie hurried to me. "Are you all right?"

I walked over to retrieve the trash can. "That dope. Watch where *I'm* going?!"

Lettie glanced after him. "Who was that?"

"His name is Calvin Benally and he's a creep."

She looked down the street again and sighed. "He seemed kind of cute."

"Cute!" I almost dropped the can. "He's a creep and a bully and he almost killed me."

Lettie smiled. "You know him better than I do, but he had a very nice smile."

I stomped over to set the can by the front stairs.

Girls!

By the time I'd emptied the cans from inside the hotel, Mom was making fry bread to go with the mutton stew. I sat down at the large, round kitchen table, took out my homework, and finished page thirty-three, problems one through thirty, in no time.

I was checking my answers when Julio Mendoza came in with a small grocery bag in his hands. "Excuse me," he said. "I just need to get our milk. Thank you for letting us keep it in your refrigerator."

My mother nodded as she slapped a blob of dough between her hands, stretching it into a large, flat circle. "I was hoping you'd be eating dinner with us tonight." She carefully slid the bread into a pan of smoking oil. Immediately, it puffed up, dancing in the bubbling grease.

"Once again, thank you very much, but we couldn't. We're already taking advantage of your kindness by staying in one of your rooms."

She turned the fry bread over. "You've probably noticed that people aren't exactly standing in line to stay here. Besides, you're working for that room, Mr. Mendoza. There's plenty to be done around this old hotel. I'll never be able to pay you for your help. You've got to at least let me feed your family.''

"We have bologna and bread," he explained. "We love bologna and bread . . . and milk." He held up the carton.

Mom's lightly browned fry bread steamed on a paper towel and another circle of dough slid into the grease. Lettie's dad licked his lips.

My mother sighed. "I guess the dog will be disappointed. He'll be stuck with leftover fry bread and stew tonight."

My head shot up but a look from Mom silenced the words before they slipped through my lips.

"Your dog doesn't like fry bread and stew?"

"He's so fussy. He only likes regular dog food." She turned the fry bread over. "I worry about him. I read somewhere that table scraps are not good for dogs, but there's no way I'm going to waste this food."

"Perhaps you can eat what's left tomorrow."

The puffy piece of bread was lifted from the pan and laid on a paper towel. Another circle of dough slid into the grease. Mr. Mendoza's tongue slid across his lips once more.

"Fry bread is best when you eat it fresh-made." My mother sighed again.

Lettie's father was weakening.

"Maybe we could save your bologna for lunch tomorrow," Mom said. "If you don't mind sharing, we'll all have soup and sandwiches."

In the silence that followed, I slid my math paper into the book and slammed it shut.

"Sharing sounds like a fine idea," Lettie's dad finally said, putting the carton of milk and his paper bag into the refrigerator. "If you're sure it's a help and not a bother."

31

"Oh, no. Not at all. While you tell Cecelia and the girls, Hobart can call Uncle Tully. This is almost ready."

Minutes later, we sat around the table, dipping warm fry bread into bowls of mutton stew. The conversation drifted from car repairs to hotel repairs to bicycle safety.

Finally, Lettie's dad leaned back contentedly. "All I can say is, your dog doesn't know what he's missing."

Lettie turned to me. "Your *dog?* Do you have a dog?"

I gave her a not-too-gentle kick under the table.

One thing I like best about my mother is that she sees dishes as a mother kind of job. She never thinks of having me, or Uncle Tully for that matter, help with after-meal cleanup.

"Let's go find something to do," I said, pushing in my chair.

"Lettie," Mrs. Mendoza said and finished with a few seconds of Spanish.

"*Si,* Mama," Lettie said.

I waited for an explanation.

"You go ahead," she said. "I'll join you after I help clear the table and stack the dishes for washing."

"I'll help." I couldn't believe I'd said it.

Neither could my mother. As the spoon she'd been holding clattered to the table, she stared at me.

Suddenly, it made perfect sense. Who wants to go find something to do if you don't have anybody to do it with?

"Two of us will finish faster than one," I said.

Mom smiled.

I could have explained that it was a completely selfish offer, but why disappoint my mother?

As soon as we could, we slipped out the back door. Before the door even closed, we heard Rosie fussing.

32

"Me too," she squealed. "Me too."

"Lettie, take the baby with you," her mom said. "I can't dry dishes with her underfoot."

"Come on, Rosie." Lettie held the screen door open.

In back of the Enchantment Hotel there are old storage buildings full of junk. One used to be a garage, another was a coal shed. The biggest one had once been a barn, complete with a now-empty hayloft. Behind the buildings, the ground slopes back to the edge of a shallow canyon, the gully. The gully's a tangle of weeds and brush and tall, old trees. It's the perfect place to take part in make-believe adventures. But not at seven o'clock in the evening when dusk is making everything shadowy and spooky.

"Isn't there a playground around here?" Lettie asked. "Rosie doesn't really know how to play anything, but she can swing."

"The only swings in town are at the school."

"I think it's too late to go over there." She picked up her little sister. "Mom will be out to get her in a minute."

"Not me," Rosie said.

I started down the steps. "Let's wander around front and see what's happening on Main Street."

Lettie laughed. "Just don't expect a parade, Rosie."

Right around the corner, in the alley, we found Lorenzo Manygoats sitting on a stack of old tires next to the hotel.

"Lorenzo! Were you waiting for me?" I stopped in surprise.

"Not really . . ." He jumped from the tires and brushed the hair out of his eyes. "I just thought . . . if you were outside, playing or something . . ."

"I'm glad you came over." I gestured toward the girls. "Lorenzo Manygoats, this is Lettie Mendoza and her little sister, Rosie."

33

"Hi." Lettie let Rosie slide to the ground. We continued walking around to the front.

"They're staying at the hotel for a little while," I explained to Lorenzo. Then, to Lettie, "Lorenzo's in my class at school."

The four of us stood on the sidewalk in silence for a few seconds.

Then, "What should we do?" Lorenzo and I said together.

Lettie sighed and looked down at Rosie. "I think we're stuck with baby-sitting."

"Me too," Rosie said.

With a smile, Lettie took her hand and led her over to the front steps. They sat down and Lorenzo and I followed.

Silence settled in again. The hotel's neon sign flickered to life and I knew Mom had remembered to turn it on for a change.

Lorenzo looked up at it.

In a minute he said, "You guys really ought to fix that sign, Hobart. People probably don't even realize this is a hotel."

I looked at Lettie and she laughed.

"I thought it was a nightclub or something," she said.

Lorenzo looked up again, trying to figure it out.

"You know, 'Chantmen,' like a band or something. And 'Hot,' like exciting."

"I kind of like the name," I said. "It's different, like a rock group."

Lorenzo laughed. "As if this town would have a rock group . . . or a nightclub." He looked at Lettie and grinned.

"A place is only as exciting as you make it," I said. "And with three of us thinking of things to do we can probably liven things up."

Lettie smoothed Rosie's hair down behind her ears. "It

might get a little livelier around here when my mom realizes that it's Rosie's bedtime.''

As though she had said a magic word, the door opened and Mrs. Mendoza said, ''Come on, Rosie. Bath time.''

Lettie picked her up and carried her over.

''No bath. No bath.'' Rosie chanted.

Mrs. Mendoza took her from Lettie and went inside. We could hear her until the door closed behind them. ''No bath. No bath. No . . .''

''Now we can really do something,'' Lettie said. ''How about a game of hide-and-seek?''

I stood up. ''Not here. Let's go around in back.''

They followed me.

''Let's set some rules. We have to stay on hotel property. You can go in the barn or the garage, but not the coal shed.'' I pointed it out. ''It's too dirty. Fair enough?''

''Fair,'' said Lorenzo and Lettie together.

I was the first player to be it. I found Lettie behind some boxes in the garage because she giggled, but I couldn't find Lorenzo. I never did find out where he hid.

''I give up!'' I shouted, and, like a ghost, he appeared next to Lettie and me.

The time went fast and soon it was too dark to see in the dimness of the buildings. Since there weren't enough places to hide outside, we gave up on the game and settled down on the porch steps. A few minutes later, my mother brought out cookies and milk.

It was nice, talking and laughing with kids my own age, with friends. I looked at Lorenzo, pushing the hair out of his eyes as he laughed, and couldn't help but smile.

Lettie Mendoza was sitting on the step with her feet up on the railing. She was a girl, and some of the guys at school would think I was nuts to be playing with a girl, but Lettie was different. She wasn't sissy or silly. She didn't try to impress people with how smart she was or how fast she could run.

I liked the way her black hair sort of curled at the ends just above her shoulders. I liked the wispy bangs that tangled softly on her forehead, and I was glad that she didn't seem to mind that they weren't smooth. I liked her laugh, the way she made Lorenzo feel right at home. I hadn't realized how much I missed my cousins on the reservation until tonight when new friends brought back those feelings.

Chapter Five

The next morning, after Lettie's father finished chewing his last bite of toast, he cleared his throat. "Leticia, your mother will go over with you to enroll in school this morning."

"I'm going to school?"

"It may not be for very long, just a few weeks, but you might as well be learning instead of wasting time."

For once, Lettie seemed speechless, but her face lit up like he'd given her a present. I'll never understand girls.

She hurried through her oatmeal and toast.

"There's plenty of time, Lettie," I said.

"Not if I'm going to fix my hair right." She smoothed some stray strands behind her ear.

"It looks just fine to me."

"That's exactly what my dad always says." She pushed her chair back, slid her dishes onto the counter by the sink, and ran out.

I looked across the table at Mr. Mendoza. We both gave a shrug at the same time. My mom and Mrs Mendoza smiled at each other.

I went upstairs to brush my teeth and double check my dictionary words for the day. Then I wandered outside to the front steps to wait for Lettie and her mom.

Julio Mendoza was at the top of the stepladder, scraping

old paint from the wooden trim around a lobby window. Uncle Tully, leaning on the "Keep America Beautiful" can, was watching him work.

"It's got to be"— the old man paused—"*dilkooh*."

"Smooth," I translated for Mr. Mendoza.

"All the paint off," Uncle Tully added.

"Right," Julio said and wiped his forehead.

As I watched, he started scraping faster, missing big areas of old, green paint.

After starting out so carefully, I couldn't believe he was doing such a sloppy job now. It was terrible.

"You missed some," Uncle Tully said.

Julio shook his head. "I've never been very good at this.'

"You missed another spot." Uncle Tully pointed. "Over that way. That's it."

Lettie's dad wiped his forehead again and sighed. "There's probably a special knack to doing this the right way."

Uncle Tully motioned him down. "Here, let me show you."

Mr. Mendoza hesitated. "Are you sure?"

"Sure."

Lettie's dad shrugged, came down the ladder, and handed the scraper to Uncle Tully.

The old man climbed up and carefully started to remove the wisps of cracked paint.

In a minute, Julio said, "I see what you're doing, but there seems to be a real art, a kind of rhythm to the job. It's going to take me a lot of practice to catch on and do it as well as you."

Uncle Tully just grunted a little and kept scraping.

"You're getting twice the old paint with half the effort, Tully," Mr. Mendoza went on. In a few seconds he snapped his fingers. "I just had an idea. We want the job done right and, if you don't mind scraping, I'm a little better at painting. I was snooping around yesterday and found some old paint in the shed out back. It's still good."

Uncle Tully was working faster than I ever imagined he could.

"Maybe I should just bring a can around here and slap some on the trim . . . brighten the hotel up a little."

Uncle Tully stopped to stretch his back. "Okay, I can get this part ready."

"You're a master, Tully. By the time I get back, you'll probably be working on that next window, then the door. I'll start painting the window trim and just follow right behind you."

Uncle Tully seemed to speed up. He started mumbling a Navajo squaw dance song as he worked.

Amazing! Lettie's father had succeeded in getting Uncle Tully to start a project. Mom and I had been trying to do that for months. As Julio started around to the back, he gave me a big wink and I answered him with a grin. Why hadn't I thought of tricking Uncle Tully into working?

Julio Mendoza's no plebeian, I thought, practicing one of my dictionary words. It seemed to me that Lettie's father was almost a prince.

It takes a lot longer for adults to get ready than it does kids. Lettie was sitting beside me on the steps long before her mother came out to join us. Adults also walk slower. By the time the three of us got to school, the crowd had already gathered under the tree. As we walked past Calvin Benally, I braced myself for an insult. Calvin didn't say anything. In fact, he just stood there in some kind of trance, his gaze following Leticia Mendoza all the way up the sidewalk to the front door.

As the bell rang, I left the Mendozas at the office and

went to class. Unfortunately, Calvin had come out of his trance. When Mrs. Buckley announced we were changing seats, he said, "It's about time! I'm dying from the air pollution around Hobart's desk. That *rez*-a-doo is powerful." He looked around. "Get it? *Rez*-a-doo? Residue?"

I hate to admit it but it was actually funny. As a matter of fact, it was the smartest thing I'd ever heard Calvin say. Only a few of the other kids seemed to understand the joke but I didn't think it was my place to explain it.

I grinned at Calvin. "I didn't realize you had such a good sense of humor, Calvin."

He studied me.

"Seriously, man, you could be a real comedian . . . like on TV."

Now he was just plain puzzled.

"I used to think you weren't anything special, just an ordinary guy, but I'm starting to see that you're a genuine *plebeian*, Calvin. Not only that, but I'll bet *nystagmus* runs in your family."

I walked over and patted him on the back. "It's an honor to be in the same classroom with you, man. You probably come from a long line of plebeians."

I glanced over my shoulder at him as I went back to my desk. He was still standing there with his mouth open. It isn't easy to work the dictionary words into a conversation. I had rehearsed how to set up the scene in my mind all the time I was waiting for Lettie.

After putting our chairs on our desks and moving things to the back of the room, we regrouped into rows, one at a time, as Mrs. Buckley called our names. Calvin was the second desk in the third row, right in the middle of the room. Maybe Mrs. B. would keep a better eye on him now.

He slowly pulled his desk forward, letting the chair slip

off, losing books and papers all along the way, stopping to pick them up, only to have them slip from his hands again.

Showoff! That clown would try anything for attention.

Finally, Calvin slid his desk into place and put his chair on the floor. Just as he slumped into his seat with a dramatic sigh, the door opened and Mr. Thomas brought Lettie into the room.

"Mrs. Buckley, you have a new student, Leticia Mendoza."

"How nice," Mrs. Buckley said, looking around the room. I wasn't sure she meant it, we were pretty crowded in there.

I thought it was great, however, and apparently Calvin shared my opinion. He slipped back into a trance.

"We're just getting the desks arranged, Leticia."

"If you don't mind, most of the time I go by Lettie." She blushed a little. "My grandmother is Leticia. I was named for her. She used to live with us before she passed away and, to save confusion, my parents decided to call me—"

"Very well, Lettie." Mrs. Buckley interrupted, looking around again. "If you'll choose one of those empty desks in the corner back there, we'll move you into place in just a minute."

Lettie's place turned out to be right behind Calvin Benally. I ended up right beside her. Poor Calvin just had to suffer from the rez-a-doo for a little longer. It wouldn't help his nystagmus at all.

I was glad to be sitting by Lettie, but I didn't get much of a chance to take advantage of the location. Most of the morning, Calvin was turned around in his seat, bothering her. The thing I couldn't understand was that she didn't seem to mind. Shoot, she seemed to like all the attention she was getting from him, laughing at his dumb jokes and smiling when he explained how Mrs. Buckley liked things done.

At recess, I met Lettie at the door. "I usually just hang around the jungle gym. It's pretty quiet out there."

"That sounds good."

It turned out that the bars weren't either one, quiet or good. Calvin Benally and his friends spent their whole recess at the jungle gym too, showing off for Lettie. If I hadn't been worried about Lettie feeling all alone, I'd have left for a more secluded spot.

I'm not sure but I think Lettie enjoyed recess more than I did.

When we started correcting math homework, our papers got passed to the left. Lettie noticed Calvin's hand signal to Davidson and shot me a questioning glance. Of course, she didn't have a paper to correct so she passed Doris's paper over to me.

"Watch," I whispered, pointing at Davidson with my lips, the Navajo way.

As Mrs. Buckley read the answers, Davidson started furiously erasing, replacing incorrect answers with correct ones.

Lettie's mouth dropped open. "That's cheating!" she mouthed. I shrugged. Maybe now she'd see the real Calvin Benally.

Right after recording homework scores, Mrs. Buckley started a review of long division. Lettie was lost. The teacher spent every minute of math time at Lettie's desk but, when the noon bell rang, my friend looked frazzled and hopeless.

"I'll never get this stuff," she said as she slipped her math book into the desk.

"Sure you will. We'll work on it together tonight."

She just blew a puff of air toward the ceiling, making her bangs bounce.

To my disgust, Calvin followed Lettie and me as far as the big tree. Then he turned the opposite direction toward his house.

"See you later, Lettie," he said.

"Bye." She shot him a smile.

I let him get down the road a ways before I mimicked, "See you later, Lettie."

She looked up at me quickly, then grinned.

After a minute of silence, I said, "You don't have to be so nice to that cheater."

Lettie looked over again. "Maybe there's a reason Calvin cheats. Maybe he doesn't know how to do the arithmetic problems."

"And maybe he's just lazy and doesn't do his homework."

"But if he doesn't know how to do it . . ." Lettie started and paused. "Well . . . I can sort of understand that because I'm lost with what we did today."

"So you're lost," I said. "Are you going to cheat tomorrow?"

"Of course not!" Her eyes opened wide, then narrowed as she smiled at me. "I'm going to take you up on your offer to help me learn it."

She put her hand on my shoulder. "Maybe that's what Calvin needs, some help . . . somebody to push him into learning how to do math."

I wanted to say, "Count me out," but I was afraid Lettie would take her hand from my shoulder. I liked the warm glow that was spreading from her hand throughout the rest of my body.

As we rounded the corner, the Enchantment Hotel came into view and we both came to a sudden stop.

"Wow!" we said in the same breath.

Even from a block away the change in the building was amazing. Every inch of wood at the front of the hotel on the first floor had been painted a creamy white and stood out in crisp contrast to the tired red brick. The change made the shabbiness of the second- and third-floor window trim even shabbier.

At the front door, *Wet Paint* signs sent us scurrying to the back. Uncle Tully was on the stepladder in the alley scraping window trim.

"Where's my dad?" Lettie asked.

The old man pointed with his lips. "*Kin goné yah iiya.*"

"He's inside," I translated, and watched Lettie hurry around to the back porch. Then I looked up. "The front looks great, *shida'i!* You guys are doing a good job."

Still scraping, Uncle Tully said, "That boy is fast. I got all I can do just to keep ahead."

"You better come in now, I'll bet lunch is ready."

"Hagoshii," he said, and started a slow climb down to the ground.

By the time we got to the table, everyone but Mr. Mendoza was seated. He came in a few minutes later in slacks and a dress shirt, his hair wet and freshly combed.

"No more paint today?" Uncle Tully asked hopefully.

Julio laughed. "You just keep scraping, Tully. I'll get back to the painting later this afternoon. When I went to pick up more paint at the hardware store, I noticed a *Help Wanted* sign at Foodtown."

He played with his water glass. "Like I told Mrs. Slim, I like working around the hotel, but if I'm going to pay for fixing up that worthless car, I need another job as well."

He reached for a sandwich. "I'm just going to talk to the manager. I'm not even sure what the job is or if I have the qualifications." He winked at Lettie. "But it's worth a try, right *mi' jita?*"

She smiled and nodded.

After lunch, Mr. Mendoza walked as far as the corner with Lettie and me. Then we turned toward school and he continued down Main to the Foodtown store.

At afternoon recess, I took out a ball so Lettie and I could play foursquare. Lorenzo and a few others joined us. Calvin and his friends wouldn't play, but they wouldn't leave us alone either. They kept racing through the square and messing up the game. Lots of kids yelled at them, but not Leticia.

"The thing is, you can't treat long division like it's backwards times tables, Lettie," I said that afternoon.

She gave a big sigh. "But that's what division is, multiplication turned around."

We were sitting at the big round table in the kitchen, trying to concentrate while my mother fixed dinner.

"But if you just use times tables to work long division, you have to do a ton of erasing and pretty soon you have holes in your math paper."

Lettie looked down at her messy paper, ripped it out of the notebook, and carefully wrote her name and the page number at the top of a clean sheet.

"It's impossible, Hobart. If you don't use times tables, how do you work the problems?"

"I *do* use times tables, but first I look at the problem as though I'm a contestant on one of those game shows on TV."

I pulled the math book closer and wrote the first problem on a piece of scratch paper. "Look, seventeen thousand, two hundred, and fifty-six, divided by forty-eight. How would you start?"

Lettie scooted closer. "Four goes into seventeen four times."

I stopped her before she wrote her answer on the page. "Try it my way." I jumped up and grabbed a big wooden spoon from the drawer to use as a microphone. Making my voice deeper, I spoke with phony enthusiasm. "Our next contestant is Miss Leticia Mendoza. Tell me, Miss Mendoza, what 'ten' number is forty-eight closer to, forty or fifty?"

Lettie sighed. "Fifty, of course."

"And how many piles of fifty could you make with one hundred seventy-two gumballs?"

"Gumballs?" my mom said. I shrugged.

Lettie closed her eyes for a few seconds. "You could make three piles."

"If my lovely assistant will place a three above the two in our problem, we'll check your answer, Miss Mendoza."

Lettie became the assistant and wrote the number three.

"Now comes your chance to use times tables," I said.

"Three times eight is twenty-four, put down the four and carry the two. Three times four is twelve and two is fourteen." She chanted as she worked the problem. "Twelve subtract four is eight. Six take away four is two. So far, so good."

"Bring down the five," I whispered.

"Now, Miss Mendoza, for a chance to double your winning, tell me how many piles of fifty gumballs you can make from two hundred and eighty-five."

Again, her eyes closed. "Five," she said, at last. "This is fun!"

She mumbled to herself as she did the multiplication, then finished the subtraction in silence. Without further coaching from me, she finished the problem. "Three hundred and fifty-nine, with a remainder of twenty-four."

"That's right! Let's hear a little applause for our terrific contestant," I said, into my "microphone." "You have not only won the first round, Miss Mendoza, you now qualify to compete in twenty-nine more contests!"

Lettie laughed and started copying the next problem. Whenever she made a mistake or looked like she was getting frustrated, I made a loud buzzer sound. "Try again, Miss Mendoza."

My buzzer call made mom jump so she was glad that I had to make the sound less often as Lettie moved through the assignment. She breezed through the last line of problems without a single buzz.

"You did it, Hobart! You taught me how to do long division! I will love you forever!" She grabbed me in a tight hug. When she let go and noticed my blushing face, she turned, folded her paper, and closed it into the math book.

My mother watched the whole thing with an amused smile.

Lettie turned to me once more. "You're a genius, Hobart. Thank you."

"No problem," I mumbled, still feeling the strength of her enthusiastic hug.

"You two get the table ready for dinner, please," Mom said.

"But, Mom, what about *my* homework?"

"You can finish it after we eat."

Chapter Six

The next morning, when we passed our math papers to the person on our right for correcting, Calvin held up three fingers. Eleanor nodded and took out her big pink eraser. Lettie looked over at me and blew the bangs up from her forehead.

In a few minutes, Mrs. Buckley called for Calvin's score and in my head I said, *Three* as Eleanor called, "Three." When the teacher got to my name, I thought, *Zero,* but Lettie called out, "Two."

"Two?" I shot her a puzzled look.

She answered with an apologetic shrug.

Mrs. Buckley asked, "Two?"

"Two," Lettie said again.

Shoot! I knew I should have taken time to check my paper over. After helping Lettie and doing all the other things that Mom expected, there hadn't been enough time. I had to fly, just to get the problems worked.

Even worse, Lettie's score was one hundred percent. She looked at me and smiled. "Thanks," she whispered. "I couldn't have done it without your help." It didn't make me feel any better.

"Let's try another page of long division," Mrs. Buckley said and a groan rose from the room. "Sorry, ladies and gentlemen, but those scores today didn't exactly sparkle. Even Hobart had trouble."

My face got hot and I grabbed the edge of my desk top to keep from jumping up to explain.

"Lettie's paper received the only perfect score. May I point out that she's not complaining about another page of long division?" The teacher flipped through her math book. "Let's use the practice pages at the back of the book. Give page two hundred sixty-five a try. Set one, problems one through thirty."

Another groan began, but Mrs. Buckley silenced it with a stern glance around the room.

Lettie leaned forward. "Calvin."

He turned around with a big smile on his face.

"Do you want some help with this stuff?"

His smile disappeared and a scowl took its place. "Not from a girl!" He turned back to face the front of the room.

Lettie wouldn't give up. "I didn't mean me. I meant Hobart. He has a way of making the whole thing clear." I tried to protest, but she went on. "He's so good at math that he makes it fun."

Calvin sent a smirk in my direction. "I noticed how good he is. I only missed one more than he did."

"Thanks to Eleanor's eraser," I whispered.

I thought Calvin was going to jump up and hit me but Lettie hurried on. "No kidding! Hobart makes math into a game. In just a few minutes, you start to understand how everything fits together."

"I'll bet," Calvin sneered. "Ho-o-bar-r-rt's a real genius."

"You don't have to worry about Calvin," I told Lettie. "He's smart enough to figure things out on his own. He's got a real *plinth* on his shoulders."

"A what?" she asked, but I didn't explain. Here was my chance to fit today's dictionary words into the conversation.

49

"I have no doubt he'll keep up his good work in school. As the years go along, the *miasma* that has started following him through life will just get stronger and stronger."

Both of them sat there and looked at me. In a few seconds, Lettie said, "Hobart, sometimes you don't make any sense at all."

"That's for sure," Calvin put in.

"Leticia, Calvin, and Hobart," Mrs. Buckley interrupted. "Let's settle down and work so that others can do the same."

In a minute, Lettie whispered, "I only wanted to give him a chance."

I ignored her. If she wanted to give him a chance, she could leave me out of it. The point on my pencil broke as I started copying the next problem. Relax, I thought to myself, just work steadily and carefully. Lettie wasn't going to beat me in math again.

At supper, no one mentioned Mr. Mendoza and Uncle Tully's paint-splattered hands. Methodically, they shoveled the food from their plates into their mouths.

Finally, Lettie's mom said, "You should slow down just a little, Julio. You're going to get indigestion."

"All the window trim is done and there's just enough daylight left to finish the porch railing in back," he said between bites.

Almost like Siamese twins, the men got up from the table, set their plates on the counter, and went outside.

Lettie and I wanted to follow them as soon as we finished. We couldn't wait to investigate the pounding noises coming from out back, but we had to clear the table first.

The strange sound turned out to be Uncle Tully, building a ladder out of two-by-fours and scrap lumber. Mr. Mendoza was busy painting. Both jobs were completed at almost the same time. Then the two men stood side by side, stretching their tired muscles and gazing at the hotel in the dim, after-sunset light. They had a right to be proud. Every inch of wood trim on the first floor of the hotel was smoothly covered with fresh, cream-colored paint. It looked beautiful!

Mom and Mrs. Mendoza came out to join the silent celebration. It was such an amazing change that we all stood at the far edge of the glow from the porch light and examined the new and improved hotel to make sure it was real.

Finally, when everything except the back porch was swallowed by the dark, Mr. Mendoza spoke. "I'll help you put the ladder up tomorrow morning, Tully, before I leave."

Standing next to her, I felt Lettie flinch. "Where are you going, Daddy?"

He put his arm across her shoulder to give her a hug. "I've been so busy, I forgot to tell you, *mi'jita*. I got that job at Foodtown. I start tomorrow morning."

"What kind of job?" Lettie looked down as the toe of her shoe traced a crack in the sidewalk.

"I'm working in the produce department, with the fruit and vegetables."

"That's great!" I said.

Lettie didn't sound so sure. "At least you won't be ringing up groceries at the front of the store where everyone can see you."

Her father's eyes narrowed as a frown crossed his face. "You don't want people to see your father working at the Foodtown store?"

She shrugged. "Well, it's not much of a job for a computer specialist."

"Leticia!" Mrs. Mendoza said sharply, but her husband held up his hand and she said no more.

Lettie's dad knelt in front of her and took her hands in his large, paint-splattered ones. "Leticia, work is work. All work is honorable if you do your very best . . . if you make a contribution to people and make the world a better place. If you think being a vegetable man or a grocery clerk . . . or a garbage collector, for that matter, is not a worthy job, you had better think again."

She continued to look at the sidewalk.

He stood up and ruffled her hair. "It's late. We should all be in bed right now."

The others started toward the door. As they moved, Lettie grabbed her father's hand and stopped him. I noticed and decided my shoelaces needed retying.

Kneeling at the bottom of the porch steps, I watched everyone go in the door. Then I heard Lettie say, "Daddy, I'm sorry. I didn't mean I was ashamed of you or anything."

Her father smiled, but there was a question in his eyes.

"It's just that . . . you . . . you're so much more than a grocery store worker. You have more talents . . . more brains . . ." She shrugged. "Are you sure you don't mind working there?"

He laughed. "My little Leticia, this is only temporary. I'm not going to work in the middle of cabbages for the rest of my life, just long enough to get the car fixed and get us to Wyoming."

He pulled her to him in a quick hug. "But I'll tell you one thing, my little worrier, I'm going to be the best fruit and vegetable man that Foodtown has ever seen."

He stood very straight, took a deep breath, then flexed his muscles dramatically. "You are looking at the Lettuce King of New Mexico!"

He laughed again. And this time she joined him.

The weekend was busy. Lettie's dad had to work at the store on Saturday, but Sunday it was closed and he worked with Uncle Tully, painting. The old man thought they should take Sunday off, but Mr. Mendoza reminded him, "This is the only day I can help you, Tully . . . Of course, if you want to do it all on your own, I'll understand."

"We better get busy," Uncle Tully said.

Lettie and I kept water and lemonade flowing to the painters.

Monday morning, right after the Pledge of Allegiance, Mrs. Buckley said, "We've been in school for four weeks and I think we know one another well enough now to elect class officers."

"What for?" Calvin wanted to know.

"To help the class run smoothly, serve on the Student Council, things like that."

I could see that Calvin liked the idea of running things. If he got the chance, he'd run things, and people, right down like a tank.

While I was picturing how bleak my life would be under Calvin Benally, class officer, the strangest idea shot through my mind. I'd be the first to admit that I've never been competitive, I've never wanted to be a person that tried to run the show. It might have been Mr. Mendoza's talk a couple nights ago about making a contribution and doing your best. But, all of a sudden, I had a crazy desire to run for office.

Mrs. Buckley was still talking. "We'll elect a president, vice president, and secretary. The president will attend Student Council meetings and conduct class discussions. The vice president will fill in when the president's absent.

The secretary will keep a record of the things we decide that affect the class.

"Look around at your classmates and think of who has the qualities to be a good leader. The person you want to nominate to be a class officer should be a good example, a good citizen. Honesty and friendliness are other important qualities for a leader. Oh, and the secretary should have good handwriting." Everyone laughed at that.

Mrs. Buckley walked over to her desk. "Think about it for a while and we'll have a nominations meeting right after morning recess. Now take out your English books."

All the time I was trying to tell subjects from predicates, the crazy idea that I might want to be class president kept darting through my head. Every time it flashed by, I chased it right out. What a dumb idea!

At recess, Lorenzo and I waited for Lettie by the door. I'd promised Lorenzo that I'd show him how a stuntman gets shot off a building.

Leticia followed a group of girls out the door.

"We're going to the jungle gym again," I said.

She looked surprised to see us, then a little embarrassed. "Dolores invited me to jump rope with some of the girls. I hope you don't mind."

"That's okay . . . Lorenzo and I have something to do anyway." What a relief! I didn't have to worry about her being alone this recess. It was great that she was making her own friends. Shoot, if it was so great, why did I feel kind of disappointed?

"We're still walking home for lunch together, aren't we?"

"Of course," she said.

Most of the time, the jungle gym is not what you'd call popular with sixth-grade kids. That's what makes it a perfect place to practice stunts.

Lorenzo and I sat at the very top.

"It's really easy," I said and stood up, bracing my knee against one of the bars. "The trick is, you can't actually *die* until after you're on the ground."

He gave the usual Navajo signal that he understood. "Mmm."

"Just watch." I moved through the stunt while I talked. "The bullet hits you right in the stomach. Jerk in your stomach muscles and kind of fall back, then double up a little and lean forward, away from the building."

"Building?"

"The jungle gym. You've got to use your imagination. Make sure you fall clear of the bars. Just jump out a little." I let myself fall forward. "Land on your feet, and stagger around a little bit. Clutch your stomach. Then fall down flat." I demonstrated, lying perfectly still for what seemed a long time.

"Is that it?" Lorenzo asked.

"The most important thing is, after you die, don't move until the director yells, 'Cut!' "

I scrambled up, dusting sand from my clothes. "If you die while you're still on the building, it'll look phony to land on your feet. That's why you have to stagger around a little before you drop."

I climbed back up to sit next to him.

"Do you want to try it?"

Lorenzo didn't answer right away, then, finally, "Maybe in a minute."

We sat without talking and watched the other kids for a while.

"You should run for class president," Lorenzo said out of the blue.

"Are you kidding? Not me."

"Why not you?" He pushed on. "You'd be a good

president. You're a nice guy. You're the smartest kid in the class.''

A kind of snorting laugh slipped from me and he grinned. "At least, in math you are. You're the best man for the job and I'm going to nominate you after recess.''

"Maybe I don't want to run for class president," I said.

"You've got to run.''

"Says who?''

Lorenzo stood up. "Says me." An imaginary bullet plowed into his stomach. He lurched off the jungle gym, hit the ground, staggered like a pro, and fell down dead. Then he looked up at me and grinned again. "Besides, you're the only kid in our class brave enough . . . or crazy enough to run against Calvin Benally. For sure, most of us don't want *him* for president.''

"Well, since you put it that way, maybe I will run." The bell rang just as a bullet hit me. I didn't have time to do a convincing stagger.

We hurried toward the building, brushing ourselves as we ran. Mrs. Buckley doesn't let you get a drink if you're late.

We caught up with Lettie at the door.

"You won't believe it, Hobart.'' She laughed. "The girls are going to nominate me for class president!''

She was right, I didn't believe it.''

"Hobart's going to run for president too.'' Lorenzo said.

"No, I'm n—''

"Hobart! If you're running, I'm not going to.''

"Forget it, Lettie. Go ahead. I don't really want to be a class officer anyway. I said it fast and loud, trying to convince myself as well as Lettie.

A mean, mocking voice broke into our discussion. "Why don't you both run?'' The three of us looked around to catch Calvin grinning at us. "No matter how many kids run against me, I'm going to win."

"You can't be sure of that, Calvin," Lettie said.

"I think I can."

I looked at Lettie and she turned to look at me.

"Come on, you guys," Lorenzo pleaded. "With both of you running, at least there's a chance that one of you will win." His voice became almost a whisper. "If neither one of you runs, Calvin will be class president for sure."

Something clicked in Lettie's eyes and I knew she felt the same way I did. "If you really don't mind," she said.

"I think it sounds like fun," I said. "You'll make a good president."

"Oh, no, *you*'ll make a good president." She smiled.

Mrs. Buckley's voice boomed through the door. "No more drinks! We have things to do!"

So Lettie, Calvin, Sam Begay, and I ended running for class president. Sam nominated himself. It turned out that nobody wanted to run for vice president, but two girls ran for secretary.

"Just like the federal government, we'll have a primary election to decide which two candidates will run in the final election," Mrs. Buckley said. "Since we have no candidates for vice president, let's have the winner of the final election be president and the runner-up take the position of vice president."

"That's fine with me," Calvin said.

Lettie and I looked at each other. We broke into smiles at the same time. Even if Calvin Benally won, we were going to give him a real race.

Chapter Seven

Mom and Mrs. Mendoza got all excited when we told them about both of us running for president. I kept explaining that it wasn't an earth-shaking event, just a class election, but it didn't seem to calm them down.

After school, they made us sit at the table for a strategy meeting, but they never quite explained what that was. They talked for forty-five minutes about posters and speeches and making our stand on the issues clear to the voters. They were definitely more serious about the election than we candidates were.

As excited as our mothers were, they were calm compared to Lettie's dad when he got home from Foodtown. He picked her up and swung her around in a crazy dance. I don't know how many times he said, "My little Lettie, class president." Then, he'd notice me and quickly add something like, "And Hobart, a fine class president himself." You'd think Lettie had already won the election.

I looked through my history book but I wasn't ready to start doing homework. My attention kept drifting to Mr. Mendoza's face and the expression he had when he looked at Lettie. It was kind of dopey but I wished I had somebody watching me with that expression, somebody besides my mother, somebody taller and stronger, somebody who worked for the railroad.

Finally, Mom said, "I'd better get dinner fixed. We need all the energy we can get."

Lettie's dad grabbed her for one last dance. "Right after supper we'll start working on campaign slogans, posters . . . Maybe we'll design pins or something."

"Daddy, we have a whole week before the primary and then another week for the two winners to drum up votes for the final election." Lettie glanced at the ceiling. "If we come on too strong the first few days, the kids will be sick of Hobart and me by the time they get to vote."

"That's my girl." He beamed. "She's got her strategy planned already."

Lettie looked at me and we both broke into a laugh.

"My strategy is to keep you grown-ups from driving us crazy," Lettie said. "Come on, Hobart, let's go find something else to do. We need to relax."

"I'm right behind you."

We ended up sitting on the front steps, watching Uncle Tully scrape paint from the second-floor window trim. It wasn't exactly fun, but it was more relaxing than staying inside with our campaign managers.

In a few minutes, Calvin Benally sped by on his bicycle. He circled back and skidded to a stop in front of us.

"Hi, Lettie," he said.

"Hi."

"What are you doing?"

"Just sitting here," Lettie said. "Where are you going?"

"Just cruising around." He let his bike roll forward slowly until it bumped into the curb.

I stood up, hoping Lettie would follow my lead. "I guess we'd better go in and get started."

She didn't catch the hint. "That's really a nice bike."

"It's okay." He pushed the bike back a few inches

from the curb, turned his front wheel toward the street, and sped off. Down the road, he circled back, bumped over the curb, and raced up the sidewalk. When he came to the alley, he jumped off the curb and flew above the pavement for a few yards.

As he continued up the street, Lettie turned to me. "Do you have a bike? That looks so fun."

"I have a bike, but the chain's broken and the tire's flat.'

"Maybe we can fix it."

I shook my head. "Not the chain. We can fix the tire maybe, but it's still no good without a chain."

Lettie looked up toward the second floor. "Maybe Uncle Tully can fix it."

I laughed. "He already told me he'll fix it, as soon as he finds time." I raised my voice. "Right, *shida'i?*"

"*Ha'at'ii?*" he said, pausing in the middle of his scraping job.

"Never mind."

Calvin was racing back toward us. He pulled up on the handlebars and rode for a few yards on his back wheel. Lettie clapped.

Don't encourage him, I thought.

Again, he skidded to a stop in front of us.

"Do you want to ride?" Maybe he wasn't such a creep after all.

"Sure," Lettie said, getting to her feet.

She rode the bike down the street and tried to jump it off the curb like Calvin had done. She wasn't going fast enough. The bike just bumped down to the street. She continued on past the hotel, gaining speed on the way back. When she stopped, she skidded too.

"Whoops, I haven't ridden for a long time." Her smile

was white against the blush of her face. "Hobart, you're going to love this bike."

Calvin grabbed the handlebars. "Sorry, I've got to get going. Maybe another time."

"That's all right," I said. "I have stuff to do right now anyway."

Lettie touched the rear fender as he started off. "Thanks, Calvin. It was fun riding a bike again."

We watched him ride down the street.

" 'Sorry, I've got to get going.' " I mimicked Calvin's snooty voice.

Lettie grinned. "Well, maybe he *did* have something to do. You're so paranoid, Hobart. Why don't you give Calvin a little credit. He was pretty nice to share his bike."

"Right. He was pretty nice to you."

She blushed.

Calvin came back later that evening after dinner and Lettie rode his bike again. I didn't give him a chance to turn me down.

As I watched him run alongside the bike, giving her riding tips, I heard her laugh. Uncle Tully had stopped scraping. He was watching Lettie and smiling. I guess he was glad she was having such a good time.

"Hi." All of a sudden, Lorenzo appeared beside me.

"Hi."

"I came over to see if you needed any help with your election stuff."

"Let's go up to my room," I said. Turning my back on Lettie and her bicycle coach, I led the way into the hotel.

"Have you thought of a slogan or anything?" Lorenzo asked and sat down on my bed.

"I've been thinking, but all I've come up with is 'Hobart for President.' "

"That's catchy." He grinned and brushed the hair out of his eyes.

"Well, help me think of something then, Einstein."

He leaned back on my pillow with his hands behind his head. "Maybe we can find some kind of a symbol to use, an animal maybe, like the Miami Dolphins. It ought to be something Indian though. How about a wolf . . . maybe an elk."

"I don't know, *sik'is*. What kind of animal would make a good class president?"

He was silent for a little while. "Maybe an animal isn't such a good idea. Calvin will find a way to make fun of it."

Another minute of silence gave us time to think. The sound of Lettie's laughter drifted through the open window.

Finally, Lorenzo said, "How about some kind of food? Everybody likes food."

"Food?"

"Something like a candy bar," he went on. "We could stick the candy right on a piece of paper with your slogan."

He grinned. "Picture this: 'Vote for Hobart, he's a *Big Hunk*.'" We both laughed.

"I've got one," I said. "'Vote for Hobart, he has *Mounds* of leadership.'"

Lorenzo groaned.

In a minute, he said. "What about gum? Everybody likes gum."

"It's against the rules to chew gum in school."

"Hobart, this is an election. The rules don't count in politics."

I shrugged. "Okay, do you mean something like, 'Vote for Hobart, he won't *gum* things up'?"

Lorenzo was already shaking his head. Suddenly, he stopped with a grin. "That's it, a stick of gum! '*Stick* with Hobart, an outstanding class president.' "

I liked it. I wasn't sure the "outstanding" part was true, but sometimes you have to stretch things a little.

"You're a genius, Lorenzo. Tomorrow, I'll buy some paper and the gum and make posters and campaign pins."

"I'll come over and help if you want."

"Thanks. That'll be great."

Lorenzo stood up. "I'd better go." He paused at the door. "How's Lettie doing on her campaign?"

I shrugged. "You probably noticed that she's using all her energy in winning a single vote: Mr. Popular, Calvin Benally."

"Yuck."

"She hasn't had much time to think about slogans or posters or things."

Lorenzo looked serious. "Maybe that's just the way Calvin wants it."

I started to laugh but the look on Lorenzo's face stopped me. Maybe he was right. If Calvin could keep Lettie from working on the election, that was one less candidate he had to beat.

On Tuesday, Lorenzo walked home from school with Lettie and me. We stopped at Foodtown to buy construction paper and chewing gum. Of course, we had to say hello to Lettie's dad, and he wanted to know what we were doing. He liked my campaign slogan.

"It's catchy," he said, setting a head of lettuce on the pile and wiping his hands on the green apron he was wearing. "How about you, Leticia? What's *your* slogan?"

"I'm still thinking, Daddy."

"Do you want some help?" he asked, a sparkle in his eyes.

"Maybe ... I'm not sure. I'm going to start working on it as soon as I get home."

But she didn't. As we reached the hotel, Calvin Benally rode up.

"Do you want to take turns riding again?" he asked.

"Oh, yes," Lettie said, then she looked at Lorenzo and me. "But only for a minute. I've got a million things to do."

I guess she decided that the million things could wait. When Lorenzo and I finished gluing thirty sticks of gum onto squares of turquoise-blue construction paper and writing my slogan thirty times by hand, Lettie was still playing with Calvin.

We didn't plan on listening to their conversation. It's just that Lorenzo volunteered to help me empty the trash cans, and just as we were finishing, the two bike riders came down the alley. Calvin was pushing his bike and Lettie was walking next to him. We didn't want to get into a conversation with King Calvin, so we ducked behind the dumpster.

"I'd better go in and get started," Lettie was saying. "It was fun, Calvin. Every time I make a jump off the curb, it feels like my stomach is flying right up to my shoulders."

They must have stopped walking, their voices weren't moving down the alley.

"I don't know how to thank you for sharing your bike with me."

"Do you mean that?" Calvin said.

"Of course I do."

"Well, there is one way you could show your appreciation."

"There is?" Lettie's voice took on a suspicious tone.

"Lettie, why don't you drop out of the election for class president "

"Calvin!"

"It's no big deal, Lettie. I'm going to win anyway. The thing is, I can beat old Hobart without even trying, but you might pick up quite a few of the girls' votes."

"Calvin, I can't believe this!"

"Now, don't get all excited. I just thought we were friends. You know, sharing my bike and everything."

"I thought we were friends too, Calvin Benally. I thought you were letting me ride your bike because we're friends. If I'd known you were just using the bike to get me to drop out of the election—"

"That's not the only reason I was sharing my bike!"

"Oh?" I could picture the stubborn look on her face. "And what if I stay in the race? Are you still going to come over? Are we still going to take turns riding your bike?"

"Of course! Well . . . I don't know. I might be pretty busy . . . with the election and everything. Of course, if you weren't running, I wouldn't have to work so hard . . . I'd probably find more time for bike riding."

There was a crash. I think Lettie pushed Calvin and he fell over his bike, slamming it against the Dumpster.

"You are a jerk, Calvin. The biggest jerk I've ever met!" Her footsteps tapped down the alley toward the back of the hotel, then stopped. "I'll tell you something. I'm staying in the race for class president."

The footsteps started again.

"I was only kidding, Lettie."

Her footsteps stopped. "I'll just bet you were! Let me tell you something else. I'm in the race to win and Hobart isn't going to be easy to beat either. Don't be surprised when Hobart and I win the primary election. One thing Mrs. Buckley's class doesn't need for president is a . . . a creep like you!''

I looked over at Lorenzo just as he turned to me. By the time Calvin had pulled his bike upright and pedaled out of the alley, we couldn't help ourselves. The laugh just had to come.

Lettie was quiet all through dinner. Afterward, she finished her homework, then sat in the kitchen, scribbling in her notebook. She ripped out one page after another, wadding them into tight balls, until the table was littered.

I was trying to check my math homework, but I sure wanted to open one of those wads of paper and see what she'd written.

Finally, her dad came in. "Working on your campaign slogan?''

She nodded.

"Any ideas?''

Her eyes got kind of watery. "Not any good ones.''

He walked over to the refrigerator and opened the door. "I have an idea, if you want to use it.''

She looked interested.

"The idea came to me because of Hobart's slogan. I hope he doesn't mind.''

Now he had us both looking at him in suspense.

He held up a plastic bag of carrots and cleared his throat. " 'If you *carrot* all about your class, you'll vote for Lettie.' ''

Neither one of us reacted.

"Get it?'' Mr. Mendoza said. " 'If you *carrot* all . . .' If you *care at* all?''

"We get it, Daddy, but . . .''

"You can attach the slogan to a little bag of carrot

sticks and hand them out as a snack at recess." He spoke louder, trying to get Lettie excited about the idea.

She glanced at the wasted paper littering the table. "Well . . . I've got to admit it's better than anything I've thought of."

Finally, a smile slid across her face. " 'If you *carrot* all . . .' "

She started to laugh and looked at me. "You know, Hobart, it's so dumb, it's kind of clever."

"I think it's great," I said.

Her father released a sigh. "Trust me, Leticia. It's a winner. The Lettuce King would never let you down!"

Lettie laughed again. It was a good sound and I joined in.

"Cecelia, Hazel, Tully," Mr. Mendoza called into the lobby. "Come on in here and help us celebrate."

He should have been honest and told them that their part of the celebration was to help with the slogan cards and carrot sticks.

My hand was so tired from writing my own slogan that I didn't want to help Lettie with hers. But, just to show my support, I peeled the carrots.

Chapter Eight

Wednesday morning, Lorenzo was waiting for us on the sidewalk.

"I just thought you'd want to know that Calvin's holding an election rally at the big tree."

"When?" I asked.

"Right now. He's giving a speech."

"What's he saying?" Lettie asked.

"Mostly he's complaining how unfair it is when *newcomers,* that's you two, push in and try to take over things."

"Are there lots of kids from our class there?" Lettie reached up and straightened her bangs.

"Seems like the whole school is there."

"But the election's only for our class."

Lorenzo shrugged. "Maybe they've never heard of anyone standing up to Calvin the way you guys are. All I know is, everybody's interested in this election . . . and Calvin's enjoying the spotlight."

"Just let him talk," I said with a grin. "The more he talks, the more he'll show everyone what a terrible class president he'd make."

Lettie wasn't smiling. "*Newcomers!* We're all equal members of the class, new kids, old kids, tall kids, short kids . . . everybody. The whole idea behind elections is choosing the best person for an office. Hobart, we need to go stand up for ourselves."

"Just relax, Lettie." When she said, "Stand up for ourselves," that might take more than a debate. I wasn't a coward, but every time I thought about using my muscles against Calvin, a tightness surged into my chest. It felt like something was squeezing my lungs so that air couldn't get inside. I took a deep breath and tried to calm Miss Mendoza down a little. "We'll tell our side in the campaign speeches on Friday. It's not going to hurt us if Calvin has some time to share his stupid ideas."

"Well, I don't like it ... and I'm going to stand right there and listen! He can say any ridiculous thing he wants to ... right to my face!"

She started off, stomping down the sidewalk.

"Hold on a minute," I said. "I don't think it's such a good idea to blaze in there and get everybody all mad."

Lorenzo had walked up next to Lettie and they both turned to look at me.

"Are you sure you don't think it's a good idea?" Lettie said. "Maybe you're just scared to stand up to Calvin."

All of a sudden I was mad. But not at Calvin—at Lettie. Who did she think she was, calling me scared?

"He's not scared ..." An uncertain look slipped across Lorenzo's face. "Are you?"

"I'm not scared ..." I started to explain, but whatever was squeezing my lungs reached down and grabbed my stomach. Actually, I think I was scared. I had a feeling that I could fight if I had to, but I wasn't in any hurry to find out for sure. I think I wasn't as frightened of being hurt as I was of making a fool of myself. I could picture all those kids, standing around listening to Calvin, all those eyes looking at us when we walked up to challenge him, all those fists ...

69

"Let's just circle around to the playground and go into school from that direction. I'm not afraid of Calvin," I repeated, "But he could get us into an argument that might turn into a fight. And everything might get out of hand. It could be embarrassing ..."

"Embarrassing!" Lettie gasped.

"And we could get into trouble ... if somebody gets out of control."

"It's more embarrassing to let Calvin say things about us and not stand up for ourselves."

She tapped her toe on the sidewalk. "Come on, Hobart. Nothing's going to get out of hand. We're just going to walk through the crowd and let Calvin and the rest of the kids know that we aren't afraid of him."

I caught up with them and Lettie went on, "I guarantee this will help our election chances."

"More than carrot sticks?"

She smiled and explained the joke to Lorenzo.

I tried to join in the conversation, but all the way to school, I couldn't help releasing my breath in one big sigh after another.

As we rounded the corner by the big tree, we could hear Calvin's voice. Suddenly, it faded away. I looked up to see what was going on. Everyone was following Calvin's example and turning to look at us. I felt like I was watching a movie with me in the middle of the scene. Somewhere there was an assassin with a rifle waiting for just the right moment. When he shot, I'd go into my dying routine, staggering around for a few seconds, then falling to the ground and playing dead until the bell rang and everybody went to class. I don't know why, but the three of us didn't stop moving, Lettie with her determined stomp, Lorenzo taking long strides to keep up with her, and me with my lagging, I-really-don't-want-to-be-here trudge.

"Well, look who's here, the new kids," Calvin said with a mocking grin.

Lettie stopped and tilted her head, looking defiantly into his eyes. I had a perfect view of this because I kept my own eyes on Lettie, not Calvin.

"What they don't know is that the rest of us have been together since kindergarten. We know each other, we like each other ... we trust each other." He glanced around the crowd. "But we sure don't know if we can trust kids we've only known for a month."

"If the rest of the kids really know you, Calvin Benally, that's all the more reason they'll vote for Hobart or me."

I heard Lorenzo laugh. I thought it was funny too, but the snort that came out of my mouth sounded like a sheep with a cold.

Calvin's face slid into an angry scowl, but Lettie went on. "Just because you've known someone for a long time doesn't make him better than someone new." I don't know how she managed it but she smiled at the other kids. "Everybody in Mrs. Buckley's class will get the chance to decide who will make the best class president. I don't think that decision will come from how many years they've known the candidate."

Calvin gave a loud, phony laugh, the kind that bad guys make in the movies. "One thing's for sure, we won't choose a *girl*. Nobody would have the slightest interest in what a *girl* thought ... what a *girl* had to say."

Lettie was about to boil over. She couldn't even think of an answer to that.

Calvin walked over to us. "What's in the sack, Leticia?"

As she turned away, he grabbed at the bag, catching the

71

top and ripping it open so that small plastic bags of carrot sticks with their attached cards spilled across the sidewalk.

Springing forward, Lorenzo slammed his open hands against Calvin's chest. Calvin's arms flapped helplessly to keep his balance as he fell back into a group of kids. They pushed him to his feet.

"You stupid . . ." Calvin swung his fist, but Lorenzo ducked.

Hurrying to pick up her campaign bags, Lettie looked up. "Stop it, Calvin!"

He was in the middle of another swing.

"Hobart! Do something!" she said.

I guess Lettie's cry distracted Lorenzo and he forgot to duck. Calvin's fist slammed into his cheek and slid into his nose.

He clamped his hands to his face, and a few seconds later, blood started dripping through his fingers.

Taking a step back, Calvin stood with his fists clenched and waited to see what was going to happen.

That short time, so full of confusion, moved in slow motion for me. I felt trapped between watching the movie and acting in it. I wanted to move, really I did. I was going to step in and push Calvin out of the way and help Lorenzo. My mind kept whirling around, trying to work out the best way to start when Mr. Thomas's voice thundered through the morning air and his bulky body pushed across the schoolyard. "What is going on here?"

The bell rang just then and kids reluctantly started to move toward the school building. I didn't blame them for wanting to stick around and see what was going to happen next. "No fighting" is about the only school rule that Mr. Thomas does something about. Even though I understood their curiosity, I hated them for it.

"We don't need the whole student body to solve this problem," the principal said. "Get to classes, *now!*"

Calvin started to walk off.

"Not you, Calvin! I have a feeling you're one of the major players in this game."

With Lettie's bags of carrot sticks on the ground and Lorenzo's bloody nose, it didn't take Mr. Thomas long to get the story straight. Calvin insisted that Lorenzo had started it when he gave him a shove, but Lettie was more convincing. The first step to fighting was taken by Calvin when he tried to grab her bag. Lorenzo was just defending her.

"Thanks, Lorenzo, you're a hero. Somebody has to stand up to bullies," she said, looking straight at me.

Shoot! I had been just about to step in, but how could I make her believe that?

As usual, with a Calvin Benally problem, Mr. Thomas couldn't figure out exactly what would be a fair punishment. He finally sent Lorenzo into the office so Mrs. Begay, the secretary, could put some ice on his nose. Then he told Calvin, Lettie, and me to go back to class and "Stay out of trouble."

"I'll expect you in my office right after school, Calvin," he said.

I did my best to stop the downhill slide my day had started into. But right after the Pledge, when those of us running for class office passed out our campaign stuff, I found myself out of step again. As soon as I pulled my "Stick with Hobart" badges from the bag, Mrs. Buckley reminded me that there was a school rule against chewing gum. I looked over at Lorenzo and he shrugged.

For most of the candidates, a piece of paper with a straight pin stuck through it was a top-of-the-line campaign badge. Because he was so sure he'd win, Calvin didn't even have that. I was the only one in trouble.

Mrs. Buckley looked out at a classroom full of disappointed faces. Finally she said, "Since this is a special situation . . . and because your slogan is a very clever one, you may give the students your badges, Hobart. However, ladies and gentlemen, I think it would be wise to save the gum for after school." She glanced around the gloomy room again. "If you can't wait, I suggest you chew very energetically throughout the coming recess and deposit the chewed gum in the wastebasket as you come back to class. The rule against chewing gum in school will not be ignored."

Lettie passed her campaign badges out next.

"Excellent play on words, Lettie, and what a wise choice of food to share with your classmates," the teacher said. "Very healthy, good for the body, and good for the teeth!"

She still had my campaign pin in her hand. For a few seconds she studied both badges, Lettie's and mine. Then she said, "I have a feeling that you students will try to take advantage of both snacks during the short recess break, not giving the vegetable the attention it deserves."

She smiled. "Let's save Lettie's carrot sticks for reading time. You can munch and read at the same time. There is no rule against carrots in school." She beamed at Lettie.

"Maybe there ought to be," Davidson whispered to me.

I met his grin with one of my own even though I didn't feel like it.

For the next hour and a half, every time I'd look at Lorenzo's pinkish nose, I'd think about what I should have done. More than once, I caught Lettie looking at Lorenzo too. Then she'd glance over at me. It might have been my imagination, but I think I saw blame in her eyes.

That made me mad. It wasn't my fault there'd been trouble. If Lettie and Lorenzo had followed my advice, we'd have slipped calmly into school and let Calvin Benally spoil his chances of being class president by talking too much. I knew Lettie thought that I had been scared to fight. Maybe Lorenzo thought that too, but they couldn't see the whole picture.

At recess, Lorenzo and I were the only two who didn't feel like chewing gum. Lorenzo probably didn't feel much like sticking with Hobart either, but we went over and sat on the jungle gym anyway.

"I'm sorry about the gum rule," Lorenzo said. "I never thought Mrs. Buckley would be so strict."

"It's still a good slogan." I shrugged. "I'm sorry about your nose."

He shrugged. "It wasn't your fault."

"But I should have jumped in there to help."

Nothing was said for a few seconds. Then I had to clear something up. "I know you're going to find this hard to believe but I wasn't afraid ... exactly. I mean, I don't enjoy pain and blood and broken noses and stuff, but I'm not really a coward."

When Lorenzo grinned, it made me feel a little better and I went on. "It's just that when you start a fight, the chances are pretty good that things will get worse, you and your opponent will get madder and hit harder. There's just no way of knowing how far things will go.

"When I was a little kid, my aunt and uncle took me and my cousins to a water slide in Albuquerque. All the way up the stairs to the top of this curvy slide, I kept thinking that I really didn't want to go down. When it was my turn, Uncle Ronald didn't give me a chance to explain. He grabbed the spongy mat from me, set it down, put me on it, and gave me a push. I could hear them laughing as the world blurred past my eyes.''

I glanced at Lorenzo. He seemed to understand the story, but wasn't connecting it to this morning's fight.

I tried again. "I didn't mind being scared by the slide, but I hated being out of control. There was no slowing down, no stopping to catch my breath so I could get ready to go on."

Silence settled in between us. In a minute I looked over at Lorenzo's poor bruised nose and decided I had to try again.

"I got in a fight once."

Lorenzo looked at me and grinned. "Once?"

"Well, it wasn't exactly a fight. There's this dog out home, Rusty. He's just a regular dog except he gets excited sometimes. Whenever my cousins and I get too noisy, he jumps around barking, trying to join in."

Lorenzo probably wondered where this story was going too.

"One day we were playing keep-away and I couldn't get the ball. The harder I tried, the more my cousins teased me and laughed. I finally got so mad I charged my cousin Travis, trying to knock him down. Instead he took the ball and ran. I chased him. All this time Rusty was barking and jumping around. As I chased Travis, the dopey dog came up behind me and tried to bite my heel. He didn't hurt me with his teeth, but he threw me off balance and I tripped and rolled into a sagebrush. That made everybody laugh even harder."

My bottom was going to sleep so I slid back a little on the bar we were sitting on. "This is the part about losing control," I told Lorenzo. "I stood up and brushed the sand off my clothes and I was really shaking. I grabbed a stick from the sagebrush, pulling it right out of the ground, to

76

hit that dog. Fortunately, my grandmother came over and held my arm before I could hit him—or anyone else. When I looked around, all my cousins were just standing there staring at me like I was crazy. Maybe I was a little. Poor Rusty was lying in the sand in front of me, looking up with wide, scared eyes.

"Ever since the day I lost control, Rusty stayed away from me. Even when I tried to make it up to him, pet him or feed him something special, he wouldn't come to me. As soon as I looked at him, he'd start to slink away."

I glanced over at Lorenzo and found him looking at me. "I don't ever want to lose control like that again," I said. "I keep practicing so I won't."

I sighed. "I guess there's a time when you can't avoid a fight, but I'd like to try everything before I'm forced into one."

He didn't say anything for a few seconds, then he snorted a little laugh. "Is that why you act so crazy sometimes, using strange words and acting like Calvin is the most terrific person in the world?"

"I guess so . . . Maybe I *am* crazy."

"Probably," Lorenzo said. "But at least your nose isn't broken."

I shot him a look to see if he was trying to tell me something about this morning, but he was grinning.

All morning I reviewed my recess talk with Lorenzo. Even if he didn't understand, I couldn't think of a different way to explain things.

At math, I got jarred out of my daydream by the teacher's voice.

". . . and Hobart," Mrs. Buckley was saying.

Some kids were on their way to the front of the room to stand at the chalkboard. Sometimes Mrs. Buckley lets us work problems up there to make sure we understand.

Because I love math, I like doing that. It's like showing off without having to show off. If I wasn't good at math, I'd hate it.

I went up and took my place.

When Mrs. Buckley read the problem I wrote it down and started working. I finished first and glanced out at the class before checking it. Lettie was waving at me and trying to tell me something.

I shrugged and tried again to get her message. She was holding up her fingers, but before I could count them, she held up a different number of fingers.

I shrugged again. I thought she might explode, so I tried one more time to understand.

"All right," Mrs. Buckley said. "Let's see how our board people did."

She's right about us being *bored* people, I thought and glanced at the problem next to mine. Poor Daniel had the wrong answer.

"Good, good, good ..." the teacher was saying, moving across the chalkboard. "Oh-oh, what happened, Hobart?"

I looked through the problem again. Shoot! I'd made a mistake in subtraction. I fixed it and turned around to scowl at Lettie. Calvin was talking with some of the guys. He looked at me and they laughed. I could guess what they were saying.

I got the next two problems right but nobody would remember that. They'd only think of the one I'd missed.

As we returned to our seats so another group could work at the board, Lettie whispered. "I was trying to tell you about your mistake."

I just looked at her.

"You should have looked at my fingers."

"I did look. You kept changing them."

"I was trying to tell you to change your answer. I was showing you the right number."

"I was just about to check my work when you started doing your crazy dance," I said.

"What dance? I just wanted to get your attention." Her face was getting red. "I was only trying to help."

"I don't need your help. I was the one who taught *you* how to do long division, remember?"

She just looked at me, her eyes bright with anger.

"Just worry about yourself!"

Lettie twisted around in her chair to look at the board. She didn't talk to me, or look at me, for the rest of the morning. When it was her turn to go to the board, she got every problem right. Mrs. Buckley heaped on the praise so much, I didn't think I'd be able to eat lunch without throwing up.

The bell rang and I shot out of my desk, down the hall, and out the door before anyone else. I didn't know if Lettie would mind walking home alone, and I didn't care!

Chapter Nine

It's impossible to stay mad at Leticia Mendoza. She keeps talking to you as though nothing's wrong. After your eardrums become numb, you forget why you were mad in the first place. At least that's the way it worked with me. It got harder and harder to ignore her continuous whisper as the afternoon went on.

As she walked past the big tree after school between Lorenzo and me, she said, "Let's hold our own campaign rally tomorrow morning."

"Are you nuts?" I forgot I wasn't speaking to her. "Calvin's already sore at us because of this morning. And, just in case you forgot, Mr. Thomas isn't all that happy either."

The principal had been standing at the door as we left the building. "Remember," he had said, "no trouble!"

Lettie laughed. "I'm just kidding, Hobart. I've been trying to get you to talk to me all day ... This was sort of a last, desperate try to get a response."

Lorenzo laughed too. "It worked!"

Lettie reached her hand under my arm to tickle me. All she succeeded in doing was making my face turn red.

"Come on, Hobart, don't be mad. I promise, I won't do anything to get us into trouble again. Come on, what do you say? I can't stand it when you're mad."

She dropped her books and fell to her knees in front of me. "I won't call Calvin Benally a worm-eating, manure-babbling, donkey-brained liar anymore . . . at least not until the campaign speeches on Friday."

I had to laugh. She was crazy.

"That's better. I have a great idea for this afternoon. Let's build a tree house."

Lorenzo and I looked at each other. Now we knew she really was crazy.

"Those trees in the gully behind the 'Chantmen Hot' are perfect for a hut. I'll bet we can use some of those boards stacked next to the garage. It'll be fun!"

"You guys will have to work on it without me today," Lorenzo said. "When my mother saw my nose at lunch, she wasn't even going to let me come back to school. I promised her I'd come right home and take it easy."

"How boring," I said.

He grinned. "It's not so bad. She thinks ice cream is good for a broken nose."

He turned off toward home and Lettie looked at me. "Well? Do you want to build a tree house or not?"

"Sure, it sounds fun. I guess you'll have plenty of time to work on it, unless Calvin shows up with his bike."

She blushed and started walking a little faster, but she didn't really get mad. I decided I liked Leticia Mendoza a lot.

"Shida'i, do you have a hammer and some nails?"

Uncle Tully looked up from the paint he was stirring. *"Ha'at'iish biniye?"*

"We want to build a hut in one of the trees out back," I explained in Navajo.

The old man stood up and stretched his back. I hated to interrupt him, but since I wasn't sure we even had a hammer around the "Chantmen Hot," I had to ask. The progress on painting the hotel's wooden trim had slowed down a lot since Mr. Mendoza started working at Foodtown, but Uncle Tully was still scraping and painting trim, one window at a time, in his usual turtle-speed way. At lunch, he'd said he planned to finish the second floor by the weekend, but he hadn't said exactly which weekend he meant.

As I followed him to the barn, Lettie joined us.

Reaching up to a splintering shelf, he pulled down a coil of rope. A cloud of dust billowed into a shaft of afternoon sun as he handed the rope to me.

"Nails is no good," he said. "*Tsin 'ii'aii 'ati' doothliith.*"

"They hurt the tree," I translated for Lettie.

We followed Uncle Tully as he picked up a board and went over to the back porch. Using the railing of the porch for a tree limb, he demonstrated how to tie the board to the tree. The rope was old and dirty but it seemed strong enough.

We each chose a stack of boards and headed for the gully. Lettie was in a hurry and wanted to climb the first tree we came to and start tying boards in place.

"It's got to be right," I insisted. "The tree has to be in the right place and the limbs have to be in the right position so the boards will lie flat."

"Let's not be too fussy, or we'll never get it built."

"If we're going to spend time making it, we might as well do it right. You don't want to roll off every time you turn around."

She sighed, blowing the hair away from her forehead, but she followed me as I kept looking.

Finally, we found the perfect place. At the bottom of the gully, there was a small clearing surrounded by huge old trees. A few yards into the grove, I found a tree with just the right limbs. Tying a board to the end of the rope, I looped the free end through my belt and started climbing up to check it out.

The climb seemed to take forever. I kept climbing into dead ends and having to backtrack. Lettie was even more impatient than I was. She did a lot of coaching from the ground, but since she couldn't really see a route any better than I could, most of the time her advice didn't help much.

Finally, I reached the branches that had looked so promising from below. I'd been right. They'd make a perfect foundation for our hut. The climb up was too hard and took too long but if we made a knotted rope ladder, we'd be able to get up there in no time.

Wedging my feet securely in a fork in the branches, I untied the rope from my belt. Then I pulled the board up and started tying it into place.

After each board was secure, I didn't cut the rope. I just lowered the free end to Lettie and she tied another board to it.

"This is going to take longer than I thought," Lettie said after we'd been working for over an hour.

"It will go faster when Lorenzo's here to help. We'd better get home for supper."

Actually, even with Lorenzo around, finishing the hut, knotting the extra rope for a ladder, and securing it above the platform took three more days. Of course, we didn't work on it every minute. We had campaign posters and badges to make and a speech to prepare for Friday.

Lettie's father brought home more "election food" for her slogans. On Thursday, she attached little boxes of raisins to a card that said, "We're *raisin* our standards and voting for Lettie." Her snack for Friday, a glazed donut, went with the slogan, "I *donut* care who's president—as long as it's Lettie Mendoza."

On Thursday, I had to resort to "Vote for Hobart—he has *Mounds* of ability." It wasn't true and the slogan was stupid, but the kids really liked the candy bars. By Friday, I was back to just plain "Vote for Hobart."

I admit I'm not much of a politician. My mom wasn't too creative about campaigning either. I know Lettie and her dad would have helped me but it was a matter of pride to do it on my own. It may have been a pretty lame campaign but at least it was *my* lame campaign.

Calvin's campaign wasn't even good enough to be called lame. He was sure he couldn't lose. On Friday, he put up a poster that said, "Vote for Calvin Benally for prisdent." He gave each kid a package of Hostess Cupcakes and everyone forgave him for misspelling *president*. Most of them probably didn't notice.

As for Sam Begay, I think he just nominated himself for the fun of it. He didn't hand out a single campaign badge or make any posters. With his mouth full of chocolate cupcake, he told Mrs. Buckley that he wasn't going to run for president anymore.

Friday afternoon, all candidates gave their campaign speeches. The girls running for secretary spoke first, and the three of us running for president were last. Calvin didn't have any notes. He said, "You guys should vote for the person that everybody knows and likes. That's me." Probably the shortest speech in the history of class elections.

The ideas I'd written down the night before got a little mixed up because I was so nervous. Mostly, I talked about how the president should be honest and fair and about standing up for our class when the Student Council met every month. Since I hadn't been here last year, I wasn't sure how the council worked. At my old school, they'd mostly set up rules about not standing up on the swings and how dangerous throwing rocks could be. The ideas really came from the teachers. Kids never worry about stuff like that.

The best talk was Lettie's. "I know I haven't been in your class very long, but I've grown to like you very much. Sometimes I think it's good to have new people come in with different experiences and new ideas. I'm not a boss-type person. I'll listen to the ideas you have, ideas that will improve the school and our class. I'll take those ideas to Student Council meetings and make sure you're represented there. I know that, working together, we can make our school better. And working together, we can make ourselves better. If you elect me your class president, I'll work to make good things happen."

Mrs. Buckley reminded us to think hard over the weekend about who had the best qualities to be class president. We'd vote before morning recess on Monday.

Being elected wasn't a life or death thing. I just hoped that Calvin wouldn't end up as class president. Lettie would make a good leader. If I lost, I wouldn't break into tears or anything, but somehow winning would show that I really belonged here, in town, in this school. I wouldn't be an outsider from the reservation anymore.

Saturday morning, we finished the tree hut. Because of the rope, there were spaces between the boards, but the platform was solid and level in most places.

"Let's eat lunch up here," Lettie suggested.

"I'll get Mom to make sandwiches," I said.

"I know Daddy will bring chips home at lunch if I ask him."

"We've got pop in the refrigerator," Lorenzo said.

The menu was set.

An hour later we sat in the hut, chewing and looking up at the leaves. They were getting drier, a rusty color replacing green more every day.

"How are we going to put walls on this hut without using nails?" Lettie asked.

"Walls? We don't need walls." I took a swallow of soda pop. "Walls are too confining, too hot in the summer."

Lettie looked over at me skeptically. "I think you're just tired of working."

"I'm not! There's plenty of stuff we can still do to make it better, but not walls." I lay back on the wooden planks. "Out at my grandma's house, every summer they build a summer shade. It's a big rectangle of logs with branches leaning against the sides and laid across the top. The tree trunk frame for it stays in place year after year, but the outside, the leafy tree branches, are replaced at the beginning of each summer. Every year, it's fresh like a real forest growing. I love that place."

Lorenzo pushed the hair out of his eyes. "There's a summer shade out home too. It's where everybody likes to be."

"The breeze kind of pushes in through the branches, making the leaves move until they almost seem to be whispering a story or a song. It's cool and peaceful . . . I think this hut ought to be like a summer shade."

Lettie had been quiet so long, I thought she was mad. But she was just busy imagining what Lorenzo and I were talking about.

In a few minutes, all of us were lying on our backs, looking straight up into the leafy ceiling of our hut and the filtered afternoon sunlight.

"I've been wondering, Hobart," Lettie said. "How did

86

you and your mom and Uncle Tully get here at the 'Chant-men Hot'? No offense, but you don't seem like the hotel management type.''

I laughed. ''That's for sure.''

''I was wondering that same thing myself,'' Lorenzo said.

''It's a long story, but simple. This guy named Mr. Marshall used to run the trading post out home when my mother was growing up.''

Lorenzo reached up and grabbed a leaf. ''I've heard of him. Marshall owned lots of places around here . . . a real rich *bilagaana*.''

''I guess so. Anyway, my mother used to help Mrs. Marshall around the house, cleaning, ironing, stuff like that. The most important thing she did was put curlers in Mrs. Marshall's hair every Saturday morning. While they were waiting for her hair to dry, Mrs. Marshall would make tea and Mom would sit and visit with her. After she'd combed Mrs. Marshall's hair and the old lady had run out of conversation, Mom would go out into the store part of the post and tell Mr. Marshall she was leaving. He'd open the cash register and pull out a five-dollar bill and offer it to her. Mom always refused the money. Mr. Marshall would try to make her take it, but she never would. Finally, he'd say, 'I'll just put it in your savings account then, Hazel.' It was the same every Saturday, year after year.''

I sat up and scooted over to lean against the trunk of the tree. ''Even after she got married and I was born, my mother still spent Saturday mornings at the trading post. Mom said helping around the house and fixing her hair weren't all that important, even though Mrs. Marshall was old and pretty weak. The important thing was the listening she did while Mrs. Marshall talked. Mom said the woman

87

was lonely, living clear out there on the reservation. They didn't have any kids, no grandchildren. Mom says that without family, it would be hard to find things to make you happy."

"I heard that Mrs. Marshall was crazy," Lorenzo said.

"Mom said she heard that too, but she thinks maybe lonely looks like crazy to people who don't understand. Anyway, to make the story shorter. Mrs. Marshall died and a few years later, Mr. Marshall moved away. We kind of forgot about them until we got a letter telling us to show up in town at a lawyer's office. The lawyer told Mom that Mr. Marshall had died and that she was in his will. The old man had written how important Mom had been to his wife and he left the hotel and a trust fund to her."

Lorenzo sat up. "So are you guys rich, like the Marshalls?"

I laughed again. "No way. The fund gives us living expenses every year but we won't be rich. Maybe, if we knew anything about running a hotel, we could make some money, but we don't."

Lettie sat up. "My dad could probably help. He's good at business stuff. If we stay here, that is."

For the first time, I thought about the Mendozas leaving.

"I hope you don't go," Lorenzo said.

"Me too," Lettie and I said at the same time.

That night at dinner, Lettie's dad had an announcement. "Guess who is the new produce manager for Foodtown? I'll give you a hint, he's known as the Lettuce King!"

"Julio, that's wonderful!" Lettie's mom said.

"It's not that big a promotion actually. Since there's only one guy working in the produce department, I'm still only supervising myself, but now I get to order the fruit and vegetables and decide what to put on sale, things like that. And it means a small raise.''

"Only working a week and already a promotion," Mom said. "Congratulations!"

I looked at Lettie and I'm pretty sure we were having the same thought. If the people at the store liked her father so much and if he started liking his job a lot, maybe he wouldn't be in such a hurry to move on after all.

Her father was holding up his glass of milk. "A toast," he said with a grin. "To the continuing success of the Lettuce King. May he soon make enough money to pay for fixing our wreck of a car so we can move on to our new life in Wyoming!"

All of a sudden, no one around the table seemed happy except Mr. Mendoza.

Chapter Ten

"The president tries to quiet the roar of his devoted public," I said, standing on top of the jungle gym with my arms spread wide. Lettie looked at Lorenzo and laughed.

"They will not be still. Nothing can weaken their enthusiasm!"

It was recess and I was trying to keep my mind off the ballots our class had filled out five minutes earlier. Entertaining my friends helped distract me.

"But wait! There *is* a way to silence the crowd, a very deadly way. As the president leans over his balcony to wave at the cheering people, one silent, unsmiling figure catches his attention. As the man pulls a revolver from inside his coat, the president's eyes widen in surprise. He turns, looking for help, but it's too late. A shot rings out above the hundreds of shouting voices, then another shot, and another."

I performed a particularly tricky backwards fall from the top of the bars, turning in mid-air to land on my feet. Then I staggered a few feet and crumpled to the ground, dead.

My friends clapped.

"What's the matter, Ho-o-bar-r-rt?" Calvin, Leo, Franklin, and the others were strutting across the playground. "Can't you keep your balance?"

"Oops, the wrong president got shot," Lettie said.

Our laugh was interrupted. "I just want you to know, Hobart, I won't hold it against you when I win the primary today," Calvin said.

"You won't hold what against me?"

"I won't take it out on you that you ran against me."

Lettie fell to her knees. "Oh, thank you, Your Excellency! Such kindness, such forgiveness . . ." She jumped up. "Such stupidity! I wouldn't count on winning today, if I were you, Calvin. It was a secret ballot, you know."

"So?"

"So kids are going to feel free to vote for the person they want to win," Lorenzo said, "not the one they're afraid of."

"Watch it, Manygoats. I might have to break your nose again."

The lung-squeezer was back at work in my chest. "Come on, you guys, lighten up a little. Calvin's probably right. Who's going to vote for ordinary, everyday students like Lettie and me when they could have a *wivern* for class president? Not just a regular wivern but a *fetid* wivern."

Calvin's eyes narrowed as he stared at me. Then he glanced around to see if anybody knew whether he was being insulted. Everyone looked puzzled.

"Face it, Lettie," I went on. "Here's a man who doesn't have to rely on his *wizened* muscles, he's got more *suet* than guys twice his age.

"Am I right, Leo?"

He looked over at Calvin for a second and then back at me. "I guess so."

The bell rang.

"Come on you guys, the new class president shouldn't be late," Calvin said, then he turned to Lorenzo. "I'll deal with you later, man."

91

They walked off.

"What in the world were you talking about?" Lettie asked. "I thought you'd flipped out, using all those crazy words."

"I just call things as I see them."

Lorenzo snorted. "And how's that? Tell us what those strange words mean."

"You mean *fetid* and *wivern?*"

He nodded.

"They're in the dictionary, if you're interested," I said. "I'll write them down for you."

We headed for the classroom.

Calvin was probably sorry he hurried to the room. He lost the primary. Lettie and I were chosen to run in the final election. Even with Calvin shooting arrows into me with his mean eyes, I was relieved. At least he wouldn't be standing up in front of the class after Student Council meetings giving his report.

In a strange way, the relief of Calvin being out of the race was overshadowed by the stress of running against Lettie. Before, it had been the two of us against him. Now, we were competing against each other.

I was clearing my desk after the lunch bell when Lorenzo appeared at my side.

"Congratulations," he said.

"Thanks."

"What's your strategy for the finals?"

"I'm all out of strategy, *sik'is.*" I grinned. "I was just in the race to make sure Calvin didn't win. I'm not sure I even want the job of class president."

Even as I said it, I knew it wasn't true. It seemed like every time I turned around, Lettie was beating me—in math, with friends, even helping out at home. Just this once, I really wouldn't mind coming in first.

That afternoon, during art, Calvin looked over at me and smiled. I hoped he was forgetting the sting of losing the election.

"Hey, Hobart," he said. "Do you want to see my drawing?"

"Sure."

It was a guy with black eyes, blood running down from his nose and lip. His arms and legs were bent at crazy angles.

"Very interesting, Calvin."

"It's you." He shot me an evil grin. "This is what you're going to look like after school."

My stomach took a little dive but I kept my voice calm: "There goes your A in art. That guy's arms are on backwards."

"Just like yours will be, when I get through with you."

Even though he'd been whispering threats to me all day, I'd done my best to ignore him. If he was trying to scare me with this latest one, he had my attention. My mind was full of injuries he might inflict with those not-so-wizened muscles. He wouldn't really break my arms and legs, would he? Probably not, but a bloody nose was likely.

Why had he singled me out as his punching bag? Lettie had beaten him in the election too. I guess even a dope like Calvin understood that he'd never get away with beating up a girl.

He punched his fist into his palm.

"You've really got me shaking," I said, hoping I sounded brave. Somehow, I just didn't feel like working dictionary words into the conversation.

The day was almost over and the monitors were doing their jobs. Kids were erasing the chalkboard and cleaning erasers, others straightening the sink area or the bookshelves. There were lots of jobs around the room. Lettie was plant monitor and, since it was Monday, she had to water the plants in the windows and spray water on them. Mrs. Buckley called it "misting."

As she passed Calvin's desk, she used her spray bottle to give him a little misting of his own. "Cool off, Calvin."

"Hey! Cut it out!"

"You're such a poor loser." She gave him a few more sprays. "Why don't you just leave Hobart alone!"

Great, I thought, now he'll be madder than ever!

He was. I could almost see the steam rising from him as he fidgeted with his friends by the big tree after school, waiting for us to pass.

"Don't let the big bully scare you," Lettie said.

"I won't." My voice cracked.

"Walk right by them. Don't talk ... unless they talk first. Then just throw whatever they say back at them."

I didn't need her to tell me what to do, but it didn't seem like a good time to bring that up. She'd start an argument. I just nodded.

"If Mrs. Buckley hadn't kept Lorenzo after school to finish his English assignment, he'd be right here with us."

Lucky Lorenzo, I thought.

Calvin grinned as we came closer. "I didn't think you'd have the guts to meet me."

I kept moving, hoping he'd be satisfied to let words pound against me instead of his fists. We walked past the group, and Surprise!, nobody grabbed us or pushed us or threw a punch.

I think Calvin finally realized we weren't going to stop.

"Hold it right there, you chicken!" he shouted.

We kept walking.

"Did you hear me, Hobart? I said stop."

If Calvin had been paying attention, he'd have known why he was out of the running for class president. Our reaction to his demands clearly showed what a terrible leader he'd make. We didn't even slow down.

"You creep! I'm going to kill you, Hobart Slim!"

I guess Lettie thought he really meant it. She started running and I followed. I'm not too sure of my fighting ability but I'm a great runner. It comes from all those chase games with my cousins out on the reservation. Lettie was no slowpoke herself.

Instead of heading for the "Chantmen Hot," she angled off to the gully. I had an idea where she might be heading and followed her lead. Thank goodness we weren't going straight home! A guy hates to have his mother witness him running from another guy. He also hates to have her witness him getting beat up. Mothers always feel like they have to come to your rescue, and that would be the ultimate embarrassment.

We ran fast and straight. I guess terror does some amazing things to your body. As I kept my stride long, inhaling cool afternoon air and blowing it out in hot gasping bursts, I didn't even seem to get tired. I thought about trying some fancy moves, but Lettie's scared glance over her shoulder reminded me that this wasn't a movie.

At the rim of the gully, I tripped over a tree root and somersaulted over the edge, landing on my feet partway down the hill without even dropping my math book. Lettie's surprised expression matched my own and I started to laugh. We kept running, but not very fast. Both of us were laughing now. Even if Calvin and his mob caught up, we couldn't help ourselves.

When we reached the hut tree, we scrambled up the

rope and reeled it in behind us. We had plenty of time, the bullies were still trying to pick their way down the hill. The exertion finally caught up with us and we lay back on the planks, breathing hard . . . waiting.

"We've got you now, you creeps," Calvin shouted.

Lettie and I sat up. "I don't think so, Calvin," Lettie said. "Just go on home before you get hurt."

"We're not the ones that are going to get hurt. We're not the ones running away like chicken rabbits."

Lettie looked at me and laughed, then to Calvin, "What exactly is a 'chicken rabbit'—some new kind of animal?"

A couple of the boys were trying to find a way up our tree. In a minute, Leo said, "This way, Calvin." He braced himself against a branch and coached Calvin and the others up into the lower branches.

Lettie grabbed a dead branch, broke it off, and threw it down at the intruders. I joined her, and soon we were grabbing at anything to slow down their climb. Leaves, twigs, even an abandoned bird's nest . . . nothing seemed to help. They slowly climbed up through the shower of debris, moving closer to the planks of the hut every second.

As Lettie looked around for something else to throw, a light bulb seemed to turn on behind her eyes.

"Hobart, if we get out on this limb, we can grab that limb and climb into the next tree. Maybe we can move over a couple of trees. It will take those creeps a while to climb down. We can stay ahead of them and escape . . . if we're lucky."

"Are you nuts?"

She was already stepping out onto the limb, balancing herself by holding on to twigs and leaves. Suddenly, she started a clumsy little run, jumped into the air, and grabbed the limb of the tree next door. I was breathless, watching her stunt.

Lettie was already moving quickly toward the trunk of the neighboring tree when I decided it was better to take a risk than stay there and get beat up in my own tree house. After all, this was the kind of thing I'd been training for all these years.

The camera was rolling!

I jumped up and moved as fast as I could over Lettie's route. I was perfect on the run, perfect on the jump. My hand closed over the branch at exactly the right spot. I braced myself, ready to pull my weight along. Then I heard a loud snap!

The next part is still a blur, but I know for sure it wasn't as graceful as the beginning. I bounced from limb to limb on my way to the ground, trying to grab something solid. All I ended up with were two fists full of leaves. Luckily, I landed on ground that had been padded with dry leaves from the past hundred years. Even with that cushion, my landing knocked the wind out of me.

Lettie gave a eardrum-piercing scream. I opened my eyes and stared into the leafy branches above. Lettie was the only one moving. She was slipping from one foothold to the next and then to the ground. She ran over and knelt beside me.

"What have you done?" she shouted at Calvin and his friends. "He's dead!"

I am? I thought. I wasn't sure what dead felt like, but my burning hands made me think it wasn't like this. I started to sit up and Lettie threw herself on top of my chest, keeping me flat on the ground.

"You murderers! He's dead and it's all your fault. When I tell the sheriff . . ."

"I'm n—" I started, and she pressed her hand over my mouth. It smelled tangy and bitter, like leaves.

From the corner of my eye I saw the attackers scrambling down.

"We didn't mean to—" Calvin began as he swung from branch to branch.

"You'll go to jail for sure," Lettie cried. "Maybe prison . . . the electric chair . . ."

They didn't stay around to argue with her. Like magic, every one of Calvin's gang vanished into the trees.

I lay still for a minute, waiting to see if Lettie would come to her senses or if I'd have to fight my way to my feet. Finally, she sat back and grinned.

"You can sit up now. Are you all right?"

I didn't move. "I'm not sure."

Slowly, I pushed myself up. "I don't know which was worse, the fall from the tree or your squishing me."

"Sorry about that. It was the only way I could think of to get rid of them."

I moved each part of my body, starting at my feet and working up, to see if anything was broken. When I turned my head from side to side and it didn't fall off, I said, "I'm glad you thought of killing me. It was a pretty smart plan."

"You did all the work," she said and started laughing.

Chapter Eleven

I don't know how long Calvin and his friends sweated, waiting for the FBI to show up and arrest them for causing the death of someone as terrific as Hobart Slim. It probably wasn't long.

Lettie insisted that I wait until after the tardy bell to show up in class the next day. She borrowed a black shawl from her mother to wear to school.

"What are you going to do with it?" Mrs. Mendoza asked.

"It's for a special project."

"What kind of project?"

"Never mind. If you don't want me—"

"You can take it, Leticia. I was just curious."

Lettie sighed. "I'd better get busy on my homework."

Later, she grinned across the table at me. "This is going to be great! It's the best joke we've ever played."

"What do you mean we?"

I decided I didn't want any part of this.

"Just leave it to me!" she said.

All evening, I kept telling her to be glad we'd escaped in one piece, but that wasn't good enough for Miss Mendoza.

"If we let those jerks get away with pushing us around, we'll never live it down," she said.

"Shoot, they didn't get away with it, Lettie, we got

away . . . just barely, I might add, through your imagination and good acting.''

"Thank you.''

"Now let's just drop out of the game and let things settle down. Those guys are probably embarrassed. If you tease them, the whole fight will grow worse.''

"Just this once, Hobart, let's make them realize how terrible it would be if they actually hurt someone. If you go along with me on this, I swear I'll never tease them again.''

The trouble is, no matter how hard you talk you can never convince Lettie to see things your way. I thought about her bargain for a minute, then said, "If you promise that you really won't bother them and you won't tell a single kid at school about the trick in the gully so nobody else teases them either, I'll go along with your plan.''

She winced. "Not tell *any*one? That's going to be tough. They looked so funny, staring through the branches with their mouths open.''

I folded my arms across my chest.

"All right, you win. If you wait to come into the room until after the tardy bell, I won't bring up the gully trick again.'' She sighed. "I hope their reaction is worth everything I'm giving up.''

I don't know how she pulled it off without explaining to the other kids but I'll bet her performance of grief before school was worth an Academy Award. When I walked in, no one fainted or anything like that. Calvin looked surprised for a few seconds. Then, squinting, he glanced around at his friends. They all shot arrows at me with their eyes.

I know how hard it was for Lettie not to talk about scaring Calvin and his friends away. I couldn't resist telling Lorenzo but I made him swear to keep it a secret. He laughed so hard he almost fell off the jungle gym.

Maybe Calvin and Raymond and Franklin really did think about the consequences of their bullying. The rest of the week, they scowled a lot but didn't threaten me. Everything just went along at a slow, steady pace. Every day after school, we spent a few minutes watching Uncle Tully work. Actually, most of the time he was leaning on the rungs of his homemade ladder, staring at the "Chant-men Hot."

Even the election seemed to have lost its fire. I guess Lettie felt the same way about running against me as I felt about her. Neither one of us brought posters or snacks. I'm sure the other kids were sorry they voted us into the finals.

On Friday, first thing after the Pledge, we gave our campaign speeches. Neither one of us was full of enthusiasm. The class voted before recess and, as we went outside, all of a sudden I just wanted everything to be over. If Lettie won, I'd be happy for her and disappointed for myself. If I won, I'd be happy, of course, but disappointed for Lettie. I couldn't remember how I got into this situation, but I wished I'd been smart enough to stay out.

When the bell rang, Lorenzo and I weren't in any hurry to get to class. I noticed Lettie took an extra-long drink at the fountain too.

Mrs. Buckley was standing at the front of the room, waiting for us to settle into our seats. Finally, she cleared her throat.

"Our class president for this year is Lettie Mendoza."
Some of the kids cheered while Lettie blushed.

"Hobart Slim will serve as vice president."

I kept smiling, but only because I'm an actor. Oh, I was happy for Lettie, really I was. She'd be a great class president . . . but the thing is, I would have made a pretty good president myself. Shoot! Nobody would ever know that I had some good ideas for making the school better. Maybe I'd done too good a job of helping Lettie make friends, of helping her with schoolwork and stuff. Come to think of it, if Lettie had never been stranded here in town, I might have won the election easily.

When that thought slipped into my head, I felt sick. Who are you fooling, Hobart? I thought. Lettie did as much for you as you ever did for her. She helped you loosen up and make friends. You started enjoying school. If she hadn't come along you never would have run for office.

Lettie glanced over at me and I gave her a thumbs-up. Her face had a pink glow for the rest of the morning.

At lunch, I knew there would be a celebration. Mr. Mendoza probably had a band waiting for Lettie's arrival at the "Chantmen Hot." Of course, he couldn't have been sure she'd win, but he'd been confident all the way. One thing I knew, I didn't want to join the party. I needed some time to myself, to get over being sorry and start feeling good about Lettie's winning. That feeling was there . . . someplace, but it was being pushed around by a bunch of other feelings. I didn't want to sit at the table with my mother and Uncle Tully and the Mendozas, choking down a grilled cheese sandwich or something, with a plastic smile on my face. My face already ached from smiling.

I couldn't think of any way to avoid it. Mrs. Buckley liked her lunch hour as much as the students did. She never kept anyone in at lunch the way she kept kids after school. Unless I pulled something truly desperate, like spray-painting Mr. Thomas himself, I'd have to go home with Lettie for lunch.

We walked out the front door and Calvin was waiting.

"I knew you couldn't win, Hobart," he said.

I just didn't have the energy to think of an answer.

"Aren't you the genius, Calvin?" Lettie said. "A real expert on *losers*."

As soon as she said it, her eyes opened in realization and her face crumpled a little with regret. I know she didn't mean to label me a loser. She wouldn't ever put Calvin and me in the same box. But, since she said it, she must have thought it sometimes. Maybe she didn't even know she thought it.

We left Calvin and walked together in silence for a minute.

"Hobart, I'm not sure if you heard what I meant back there," she finally said. "I don't think I even *said* what I meant."

"I know what you meant."

"Thank goodness. It sounded so . . . wrong, if someone didn't understand, he might be mad."

"I'm not mad. There's no problem, Lettie."

"I'm glad."

"Losing a class election isn't like losing something important, like ten dollars." I stopped talking. If winning wasn't so important, why was I feeling so bad?

She looked over at me. "You didn't lose, anyway. You're vice president."

Suddenly, I really felt like I'd lost.

The scene at home was everything I expected and worse. Lettie's dad was there. He must have made special arrangements. Except for Saturdays, he hadn't been home for lunch since he started working at Foodtown. I knew he'd been pretty sure of her winning. At the news of her victory, he picked her up and swung her around. Everyone crowded up to congratulate her. Then they all seemed to think of me at the same time. It would have been easier if they'd all kept celebrating for Lettie, but they worked hard to make me feel better. It made the whole meal seem strange. I didn't need their sympathy.

When I was small, sometimes I'd put my boots on the wrong feet. Walking around that way would feel a little strange but not uncomfortable enough to make me change them to the right feet. I felt the same way during lunch.

"You two will make a great team," Mom said.

"I've got some ideas we can work on already," Lettie said.

"Oh?"

"One thing we could do to make the school better is clean up the schoolyard."

"That's a good idea," her father said.

"We'll spend a few recesses working on it. If we make each class in the school a team and assign each team a part of the grounds to clean, it won't be such a big job."

Who wants to spend recess cleaning up? I thought.

Lettie went on. "Hobart's my right-hand man. I want him to be the foreman and take charge of organizing the teams."

I didn't say anything. I smiled.

If I'd done what I felt like doing, I'd have jumped up and shouted, "I don't want to be your right-hand man! I don't want to be anyone's right-hand man. I don't need a charity job, Miss President. You're the leader, so lead! Don't think you have to make some position for me so I'll feel better. I don't need it!"

But instead I smiled and Lettie smiled back.

The rest of the day, while everyone else was reading in their health books or listening to Mrs. Buckley talk about the Greeks and Romans, I was thinking about more important things. One minute, I'd be feeling proud that I'd helped Lettie learn how long division works. The next minute, I'd hate her for smiling over at me like nothing had happened, like she hadn't been elected president, while I'd come in last. Then I'd remember how her quick thinking had saved me from getting beat up by Calvin and his friends. In the middle of feeling grateful, I'd want to go over and punch her for offering me the foreman's job in her brilliant cleanup plan. My mind flipped back and forth all afternoon. Congratulations, Lettie, you'll make a great class president! Don't look at me, Leticia Mendoza, a real friend wouldn't have run against me in the first place!

By Saturday evening, after avoiding everybody all day, especially Lettie, I was feeling much better. I think I was actually happy for her. I didn't really want to be class president anyway, I told myself. And I believed it.

Supper was good. We had Navajo tacos, and that's my favorite meal. They're just like the tacos at Taco Bell, except we use fry bread instead of a tortilla. No one mentioned the election, and Uncle Tully told a funny story in Navajo. When my mom translated it for the Mendozas, it wasn't quite as funny, but they laughed anyway. A lot of what's funny in Navajo stories depends on playing with words. We have lots of words that sound the same but they mean something different.

My old uncle was in a very good mood. I thought it might be because Lettie's dad was going to help him finish painting the trim on the top floor on Sunday. With any luck, he'd be back to being the *unhandy* handyman by Monday.

When we finished eating, he stood up and stretched. "Everybody out to the porch," he said.

We looked at one another.

"Come." He stood up and led the way.

When we were all out on the porch, he smiled and said, " *'At'ah. T'aa akoon dasoozi.* "

"We're supposed to wait here," I translated for the Mendozas.

Feeling kind of foolish, we all stood there and watched Uncle Tully walk over and disappear into the barn. In a minute, he came out, wheeling a bicycle.

It wasn't a new bike, but the tires were new and the fenders, red in front and green in back, had been cleaned. There was an old light at the front, but it was broken. The chain was oiled and tight though. It looked like a pretty good bike to me.

"For you, *at'eed yazhi,*" Uncle Tully said, looking at Lettie.

My mother put her hands on Lettie's shoulders and gave her a gentle push toward the steps. "It's yours."

"Mine? You're kidding!"

"I seen you ride the boy's." Uncle Tully didn't say more.

Mom smiled at me. "You should get your bike, son. You two can take a ride together."

She'd forgotten all about the flat tire, the broken chain. For months I'd been nagging Uncle Tully. He kept saying, when he found the time he'd get it fixed, but he never found the time.

"Go on," Lettie's dad said to her. "Try it."

As she swung her leg over and got ready to pedal off, he turned to Uncle Tully. "I don't know how to thank you."

The old man was still standing beside the bike, and Lettie leaned over to give him a hug. "Thank you, Uncle Tully. This is the best surprise I've ever had in my whole life!"

The old man shrugged and stepped back.

106

"You'd better get going, son, if you're going to catch up with her," my mother said.

"But, Mom . . ."

"I've got to get the dishes done." She turned and was through the door and into the kitchen before I could remind her that my bike didn't work.

"I'll help," Mrs. Mendoza was saying as she followed Mom inside.

"Tully, let's take a look at that top floor. What's the best way to get at it with brushes and paint?" Mr. Mendoza said, putting his hand on the old man's shoulder and nudging him toward the alley. "I'm thinking it might be easier to come from the roof . . ."

They disappeared around the corner and I looked down into Rosie's big black eyes.

"I guess it's just you and me, Rosie Mendozie," I said. "We're the only ones with nothing to do and no place to go."

She smiled. "Not me."

Even though I didn't feel like it, I smiled. "No, not you. I'm the only loser around here. I'm the one who lost the election . . . who keeps missing easy math problems . . . who jokes around instead of smashing Calvin Benally's face in. I'm the one with a worthless bike."

Even though it was getting dark, I wandered over to the garage and went inside. Rosie followed me. There was my bike, leaning against the rough boards of the wall.

I felt like picking it up and throwing it against the back of the garage. I wanted to slam a big hammer into it, snapping the spokes and denting both fenders. If I could, I thought, I'd rip at it with my bare hands until I'd worked out all the ugly feelings throbbing inside me, transforming the bike into a twisted pile of rusted metal and worn-out rubber.

I looked over at Rosie. She was watching me with her little arms folded across her chest. All of a sudden I knew I wouldn't trash my bicycle with her there.

"Shoot," I said, giving it a kick. It wobbled backwards a few feet, teetered, and fell against a pile of empty paint cans that Uncle Tully was going to dispose of someday. The cans clattered against one another as they skidded across the dirt floor. I walked over and kicked the bike's flat tire.

Rosie was right behind me. She stepped up and kicked the tire too. "Shoot," she said.

I had to laugh. "It's not so easy to feel sorry for yourself with you around, Rosie Mendozie . . . but I'm doing my best."

"What's going on out here, *Shiyazh?*" Mom said, surveying the scattered cans.

"Nothing," I said.

"Is everything all right?"

I made myself nod. If she couldn't tell things weren't right, I didn't want to break the news to her.

"I thought you were going to ride bikes with Lettie."

Did she hear the tiny snap that signaled the disappearance of my self-control? I walked over and kicked my bike again. "Look at this piece of junk, Mom! How can I ride it? The tire's flat! The chain's broken! It's a stupid piece of junk!"

There was real surprise in her voice. "I didn't know that."

"You did, Mom. It's been broken since we moved here. I've told you a zillion times."

"I'm sure Uncle Tully will—"

"He won't!" I shouted the words and Rosie started to cry but I couldn't stop. "I've told him *two* zillion times! He's never going to find the time to fix it! He's too busy

108

fixing up a new bike for the class president! I know I'm only the vice president—Lettie's right-hand man—but that should at least qualify me for a stupid chain and a stupid patch for my stupid flat tire!''

"Maybe Lettie's father will—"

"I don't want him to fix it." I started crying. "I want . . ." I'm glad I didn't tell her what I really wanted. She couldn't do anything about it anyway.

I wanted my own dad to fix it. I wanted a dad to help me celebrate being second. I wanted someone like Mr. Mendoza to cheer for me once in a while. Most of the time it was great being just me and mom but sometimes . . . My dopey sounds of crying joined Rosie's in the silence of the garage for a minute. Then I rubbed my eyes. Thinking about my father was just dream stuff. I knew that.

As I stood there, feeling bad because I'd lost control, somehow I felt good too. I felt lighter, like I wasn't so crowded inside myself anymore.

I wiped my nose on the back of my hand and started out of the garage. As I passed her, Mom reached for me, but I dodged away and kept walking.

"Tomorrow, I'm sure you and I can—" Mom began, but I didn't stop.

"It doesn't matter, *Shima*. I don't want it fixed now. I don't ever want to ride my stupid bike again."

Chapter Twelve

Nobody bothered me the rest of the night, and Sunday morning I slept in. When I came down to fix myself a bowl of cereal, Mom was the only one in the kitchen.

"Are you all right, *Shiyazh?*" she asked.

"I'm fine," I said.

I hoped she wouldn't talk about my bike and she didn't. Sometimes she seems to know about things like that.

Every day for almost two weeks, I watched Lettie ride her bike and I stayed mad. She offered to let me ride, but I always told her, No thanks. A couple of times she said, "If you don't want to share, let's fix your bike so we can ride together."

"I've got other stuff to do."

"Maybe my dad or Uncle Tully will help us fix it."

"Forget it, Lettie, it's not that important."

But it was. I knew it was crazy but I enjoyed suffering more than I would enjoy riding Lettie's bike.

I only talked to Lettie when I had to. As a matter of fact, I didn't talk to anyone unless I had to. Of course, everybody was pretty busy anyway. Uncle Tully finished painting the hotel trim, with a little help from Lettie's dad. Mrs. Mendoza helped my mother and took care of Rosie. Mr. Mendoza worked overtime and applied almost every dollar he earned toward car repairs. He wanted to pitch in on food, but Mom had it all written out to show that he hadn't used up the credit he had earned helping Uncle Tully paint. Lettie worked hard and kept getting good scores in school.

Every day kids were waiting for her to play at recess. She got invited to walk home with different groups but she always turned them down. Even if our walks together were silent, she stayed with me. And after school, she rode her bike.

If Mom or Uncle Tully noticed I wasn't riding *my* bike, the one still lying in the middle of old paint cans with a broken chain and flat tire, they didn't mention it.

The one good thing that happened is we rented rooms at the hotel on three different nights. Maybe that's three good things. It made Mr. Mendoza and Uncle Tully feel terrific about all the work they'd done. It made me feel good because we had dessert after supper all three nights, sort of a quiet celebration. I hoped that dessert on renting nights would become a tradition. I also hoped business would keep improving.

Thursday afternoon, after emptying the trash, I turned away from the Dumpster and almost stepped on Lettie.

"Let's do something fun," she said.

"I'd better not. I have homework."

"No, you don't, I saw you finish it right after school."

I blushed. "I'd better check it over."

"Come on, Hobart. We haven't done anything together for over a week." She pulled the trash can from my hands and started carrying it back to the front. "How come you're mad at me?"

"I'm not mad . . . I've just been busy."

She snorted a laugh, then blew the bangs up from her forehead.

111

I followed her down the alley. "All right, let's do something fun. What do you want to do?"

She whirled around. "Let's call Lorenzo and go to the hut."

I had to admit I was tired of being mad. The thought of sitting on the warm, rough boards, talking and laughing, was tantalizing. We hadn't been there since my famous Tarzan stunt fell through.

"Okay," I said and grinned. She answered me with a relieved smile. At least we were talking again.

We met Lorenzo at the edge of the gully and headed down. An excited tingle seemed to have grabbed hold of me. From the easy way Lorenzo and Lettie were laughing and talking, they must have caught the same tingle. But long before we got to the tree, we could hear the noise of other kids and we recognized their voices. Somehow we knew where they were too. Calvin and his friends were at our tree house!

Lorenzo's hand rested protectively on his nose for a few seconds. "What should we do?"

The tingle quickly drained from me and a gloomy dread slid in to take its place. Lettie started off through the bushes toward the noise. "Who do those guys think they are, taking over our hut?"

Lorenzo and I looked at each other, then we followed her.

Angry sparks kept flashing up inside me but a familiar tightening in my chest blew them out like birthday candles. Leaves and branches whipping past and my feet crackling into dry leaves pounded in rhythm with the buzzing alarm in my head.

You're heading straight for a fight. If you'll just stop and think, there's a way to avoid it. As the thought limped through my mind like a mistreated dog, I hurried to keep

112

up with Lettie. I knew there was no way she would ever stop and think.

We burst through the brush into the little clearing. "What are you guys doing in our hut?" Lettie shouted.

Calvin and his friends were suddenly silent.

"Well?" Lorenzo stood with his fists on his hips. "You heard her . . . What are you doing in our hut?"

Calvin's smug face peered over the edge of the platform. "I don't see any name on this place. What makes you think it's yours?"

"We built it!" Lorenzo and Lettie said in unison.

"So?"

"Uh, think about it, you guys," I said trying to cool things down. "The hotel is right up at the edge of the gully. This is on my property." I wasn't sure that was true but it sounded good.

"Don't be stupid, Hobart, nobody owns the gully."

My heart was pounding so loudly I could feel it in my throat. Two feelings kept stomping around inside me, bumping into each other and making me feel like I needed to sit down. Dark gray fear moaned, *If it starts, you won't be able to stop it. You'll get hurt. Worse than that . . . you'll lose control of things and embarrass yourself.* Then red and orange anger flared up. *Who cares?! You're sick of things not turning out the way you planned. If you want to, you can grab the rough bark of this tree trunk and shake it until they all fall out and thud to the ground.*

The feeling of dread slid in, hosing down my anger's fire. "The boards are ours," I said, "the rope . . . We spent all the time . . . did all the work." I wanted my voice to sound calm and reasonable but, even to my own ears, I sounded like a coward.

Lettie took over. "Now you creeps get out of there . . . Get lost!"

113

Calvin looked around at the others and his grin grew wider. "I guess you're just going to have to *make* us leave."

The three of us stood there for a few seconds wondering how we could do that. Lettie's glance was darting all around, her mind working overtime. Finally, she laughed.

"Never mind, Calvin, you guys go ahead and play up there. We don't mind."

Lorenzo stared at her. "Are you crazy?"

She laughed again and started walking slowly across the clearing.

"Go ahead, stay up there as long as you want," she called.

"That's what we're planning to do," Calvin called back with a smirk.

"Lorenzo and Hobart and I would rather play down here anyway . . . with this nice bike!"

I couldn't believe it. Calvin's new bike was lying at the edge of the clearing. He must have dragged it all the way down to the bottom of the gully. What a lot of work! I guess he really liked that bike.

"Hey, get away from there. That's my bike!"

Lettie was lifting it up. "Really? I don't see any name on it."

She started pushing it off through the brush, picking up speed as she chose the smoothest course. Lorenzo and I didn't know what her plan was, she probably didn't have one, but we ran along for support. There was a racket of twigs and branches snapping behind us.

Still in the tree but clambering quickly toward the ground, Calvin roared, "You guys are really going to get it!"

Lettie laughed. "We've already got it!"

The little alarm in my head flashed its warning message

114

again. We were going to get flattened. But, somehow, I didn't let myself think about it. At least the creeps were out of our tree house.

It didn't take them long to catch up. By the time I thought of a plan—abandoning the bike, circling back, and climbing up into the hut—the boys had surrounded us and Calvin was jerking the bike away from Lettie. He gently rested it down on the fallen leaves, then turned.

"I should kill you guys for stealing my bike!"

I found my tongue again. "That's just the way we felt when we saw you in our hut."

"That's different, everybody knows my bike."

"And everybody knows we built the tree house."

With his fists clenched, Calvin walked toward me. "Now everybody knows you're going to need a doctor!"

All of a sudden, I was tired of being afraid and I was tired of being in control. Even if he broke my nose and made my head spin around like a character in a cartoon, I wasn't backing down. I clenched my own fists and raised them up like they do in the movies.

I guess I'm going to have to look for another career when I grow up. I seemed to be losing my grace as a stuntman. Calvin moved into range and I sprang forward to meet him. As I swung my right fist, my feet slid across the fallen leaves and I sort of flew into the air. My fist didn't connect with Calvin at all, but somehow my right arm got wrapped around his neck and we both rolled into the bushes.

The next thing I knew, I was flat on my stomach with a couple of leaves in my mouth. Calvin was sitting on my back. I set my feet and hands to push up and roll him off, but before I could move, I heard a thud and he was lying beside me.

At first I thought Lorenzo had come to my rescue, then

115

I heard a familiar voice. "You leave him alone, Calvin Benally!" I twisted my head around to look where Lorenzo had been standing. He was still by the bike, his mouth wide open. I rolled over on my back and looked up. Lettie's fingers were tangled in Calvin's hair and she was pulling him to his feet. She punched him in the head and he backed up. As she punched him again, I noticed all his friends standing around, along with Lorenzo, too surprised to move.

Calvin took a big step back and tripped over a tree root. At the end of his fall, I heard his head hit the trunk. I guess that took the fight out of him.

His friends hurried over to help him up. Breathing in quick gasps, Lettie watched with her fists still clenched. Calvin walked over to the bike and lifted it upright. The group started moving away and I stood up, brushing dirt and leaves from my clothes.

Calvin turned back and snorted out a laugh. "Very good, Hobart. You're really tough, aren't you . . . as long as you have a *girl* around to do your fighting!"

His friends laughed.

"Just wait till everybody hears that Hobart Slim has his very own bodyguard."

They started off again.

"Wait till they hear that it's a *girl!*"

My face was hot, but it wasn't from anger. I felt like I was shrinking so fast that I might disappear under a dry leaf. Shoot! I was going to fight! I was fighting! I wasn't backing off!

I looked over at Lettie. With her face still crunched into an angry scowl, she watched them walk away. Then, as she turned to me and noticed the expression on my face, her eyes opened wide.

I wanted to shout at her. *Lettie, how could you? I*

wanted to walk over and punch her myself, hard, in the face. *I would have done all right on my own. Why do you always push your way in?* I wanted to run after Calvin and try to get the fight started again.

But I didn't do any of those things. I turned the other way and ran blindly into the trees.

It seemed like I wandered in the gully for hours, but it wasn't really that long. At first, I planned to stay down there until I'd solved my reputation disaster. While pushing my way through bushes and around fallen trees, I planned to neatly package and label everything that had happened to me in the last couple of months. Then, after I'd stacked each incident carefully in my mind, I'd be ready to figure out what to do about my latest problem.

After about ten minutes, I knew it was hopeless. Lettie and Lorenzo and Mrs. Buckley . . . even little Rosie kept tumbling through my thoughts and getting all twisted up in a crazy traffic jam. Every few seconds, Calvin and his friends would pop up and laugh, jeering wickedly about my *bodyguard*. Finally, I stopped thinking and just wandered.

Through the magic of imagination I became a misunderstood Indian cavalry scout bringing peace to Mother Earth. While I was sneaking out of camp to contact help for my pinned-down comrades, a sentry mistook me for the enemy, firing a bullet that lodged in my right thigh. I limped on, holding the wound tightly to slow the steady flow of my brave blood.

At the top of a small hill, the renegades spotted me and an arrow thudded into my right shoulder. Leaning against a tree for support, I pulled the arrow from my ragged, bleeding flesh.

I pressed on, my right hand grasping my right thigh and

my left hand pressing savagely against my right shoulder. I was a warrior without a friend. Each side had misunderstood and misjudged me, but I would not abandon my mission!

After a few minutes, I got sick of being a scout. I was hungry and I turned back toward the "Chantmen Hot." It was still pretty early but as I came up over the rim of the gully and made my way between the garage and the barn, I could smell dinner. The Mendozas' old station wagon was parked in front of the garage. Mr. Mendoza must have paid off the repairs. I felt like climbing in, hot-wiring it, and driving away. I didn't care where I went as long as it wasn't within a million miles of Leticia Mendoza. Of course, I wouldn't really do that, I don't know how to hot-wire a car. Even if I could get the car started, I don't know how to drive.

I made my feet keep moving toward the back door.

Everyone was sitting around the table. When I opened the door, they stopped talking and looked over at me. Mr. Mendoza was holding up his water glass.

"Hobart! You're just in time. Lettie told us you'd probably be back soon."

Of course she'd told them that. And here I was. Lettie Mendoza knows everything!

At least she hadn't told them about Calvin, about my unique approach to fighting, about her amazing skill at humiliating me. Good.

As I moved to my place and sat down, she gave me a hopeful, questioning look. I turned my head. If I had to, I'd share a table with her, but I didn't want any eye contact.

"As I was saying," her father said. "Here's to the new and improved Mendoza motor car. In a very short time, I'm hoping it will whisk us to Wyoming with no further trouble!"

118

Everyone raised their water glasses, like they do in the movies, everyone but Uncle Tully. He glanced around at us, shook his head, and chuckled.

Then we started eating.

"What did the men say, Julio?" Lettie's mother asked.

"The men?"

"You know, the men from Foodtown . . ." She waited. "The management team . . . from the main office?"

Mr. Mendoza quietly studied his glass of water. He examined it so closely that I thought he must have found something floating in there. I started studying his glass myself.

He cleared his throat. "They're going to build a new Foodtown here."

My mom looked up. "Here? In this town?"

"That new federal water project is supposed to have this area booming by next year. New housing for workers . . . new recreational sites for tourists . . . A big new supermarket is going to be a necessity."

Julio was looking at his glass again.

"I'm not so sure I'll like living in a real *city*," Mom said.

Lettie perked up. "Well, *I* sure would."

Her father cleared his throat again. "They offered me a job."

Everyone looked at him.

"You have a job, Daddy."

He allowed a tired grin to play with his lips. "I mean a different job . . . a management job. Not just Lettuce King, but something at the top level, working with computers on inventory and ordering. Of course, it would just be at the store level at first . . . but, later on . . ."

Lettie's mom inhaled quickly, a tiny gasp of surprise. "It's true?" she asked.

119

Her husband shrugged. "It's not on paper, but they seemed to like me. I had some pretty good ideas about letting computers simplify their operation."

Lettie stood up so fast, her chair tipped over. She whirled around and danced over to throw her arms around her father's neck. "Daddy, we could stay here! We could have a real house again, not a bunkhouse at the ranch."

"A trailer," her father corrected.

"You could do something ordinary instead of being a computer cowboy! I could stay in school and I'd still be class president and . . ."

She was so excited and she kept talking so fast that I forgot about being mad at her again. Pictures of Lettie and Lorenzo and me kept popping into my head . . . fixing up the tree house . . . all three of us riding bikes together . . . meeting famous movie stars who came to town to get away from their frantic Hollywood lives, actors and directors and . . . stuntmen . . . all of them staying at the "Chantmen Hot."

All the time Lettie was dancing around the room, chattering about this *real* job being just about the best thing that had ever happened to the Mendoza family, her father was quietly studying his glass of water.

Chapter Thirteen

As soon as we finished eating, I went out on the back porch. I needed a quiet place where I could think. I leaned against the railing, watching the gully grow darker, shadows stretching from trees and doorways until they blended into one another. As evening seeped through my tee shirt, I folded my arms for warmth. How was I ever going to face the kids at school after Calvin got through retelling his story a thousand times? I felt like crawling into bed, burrowing down under the covers, and never coming out.

Since I might be spending the rest of the night out there, I decided to go in and get my jacket. As I reached the door, I could hear dishwashing sounds and voices. Looking through the filmy curtain on the door's window, I saw Lettie and her dad at the sink. Julio Mendoza was actually doing dishes!

I didn't want to face Lettie, so, rubbing my arms for warmth again, I went back to the porch railing. Maybe they'd be finished soon.

A few minutes later I heard the door open. It was Lettie.

"I brought your jacket. It's pretty cold out here." She held it out toward me and I took it.

I wanted to say thanks, but my voice wouldn't let me.

"I just want you to know I'm sorry, Hobart."

I turned away to look out through the darkness to where the gully would be.

"I'm really, really sorry." She walked over to stand next to me. "I just couldn't stand to see you get hurt."

I stepped away. "You didn't have to save me, Lettie. I can take care of myself."

She sighed. "But you don't."

"What makes you the expert on everything?" I said and turned to look out into the darkness again.

"I'm not an expert. I don't know everything."

I snorted. "That's right, so just keep out of my business."

For a minute the silence was like a wall between us.

As I thought of an answer to Lettie's comment about my not taking care of myself, I felt like a heavy rock fell off my shoulders. For just a second I understood myself a little better. In the thrill of that understanding, I let go of being mad at her.

"You're wrong, Lettie. I do take care of myself. I just don't do it your way."

The silence settled in again but it wasn't thick. Lettie was thinking. "Hobart, your way is so . . ."

If she said stupid, I was going to throw her off the porch.

". . . different," she said slowly. She shivered and I offered my coat, but she shook her head.

"I can't stand bullies," she said. "If you don't knock the meanness out of them, they never change."

"Who says? Who says you can't joke it out of them? Who says you can't be so darned friendly to them that they throw up and get rid of their meanness that way?"

She smiled. "Okay, you could be right. I'm the one who says you have to punch them in the nose. I've never tried it your way."

"I don't want you to try it my way."

122

I stepped over so we were side by side again. "I just want you to let *me* try it my way," I said.

Lettie blew the bangs up from her forehead. "When I was socking Calvin, I thought I was doing it for you. I guess I was really doing it for me, wasn't I?"

I shrugged.

"I made things worse for you." She waited for me to tell her it wasn't true.

I shrugged again.

A noisy truck rumbled down Main Street on the other side of the "Chantmen Hot."

"It's funny," I said. "Down there in the gully, I was ready to try to cure Calvin's meanness your way." I had to grin. "I wasn't doing it very well, but that was my plan. You didn't give me much of a chance to put the plan into action. Sometimes you have to let someone do something on his own, even if it means he gets hurt."

Lettie shivered again. "How can I make it up to you? How can I help?"

"There you go again."

She laughed.

"I'll think of something myself," I said.

She walked over and pulled open the screen door.

"Lettie?"

She paused and looked at me.

"Since you beat up Calvin . . . maybe all I need to do is beat you up and my reputation will be saved."

Her eyes widened, then she saw my grin and answered with a smile. "I'll do anything to make it up to you, Hobart."

"Good night, Lettie."

The screen door closed, then the inside door, and I was alone. Now maybe, in the silence of the porch, I could think of something.

The door opened again and Julio Mendoza stepped out.
"Are you all right, *hombre?*"

I nodded.

"Lettie told me about her . . . mistake."

That's just great! I thought. Now he thinks I'm a wimp too. Let's take out an ad in the *Navajo Times* so the whole world will know!

He walked over to me. "I know she didn't mean to mess things up. She just rushes into things too fast." I nodded again.

"Sometimes that's not a bad way to be. If you're willing to take some risks and dive right into things, it usually works out okay. I don't think you'd want to be on high speed all the time, but at least you don't end up regretting that you didn't try."

He leaned against the railing and took a deep breath. "I guess Leticia got a lot of that craziness from me, but I sure seem to have lost it." Another deep breath. "I wasn't going to tell them about the job at Foodtown, you know . . . Lettie and her mother. I knew they'd like the idea of settling down right here in town, it seems to be safe and more . . . normal than ranching."

All of a sudden, I realized he wasn't talking to me anymore. He was just thinking out loud.

"The supermarket job is more secure. I know that . . . but I was looking forward to the ranch, trying something new, something with a little adventure in it.

"When a man has people depending on him . . . a wife and two little girls, I guess he ought to skip the adventure and go with something safe."

He noticed me standing there. "But what if, in a few years, we start to wonder how it might have been if we'd gone on to Wyoming like we'd planned?"

I gave another nod.

"You just don't know, if you don't take the risk, if you don't try something new, do you? The crazy something might just turn out to be better than the safe something."

We were silent for a few seconds. Then I said, "We had to memorize poems in school last year. Some of them were by this guy named Langston Hughes. I liked all his poems, but my favorite was called 'Dreams.' "

Mr. Mendoza looked over at me with a puzzled expression. I know he thought I'd taken a U-turn in the conversation. Before he could interrupt, I started quoting the poem.

> *Hold fast to dreams*
> *For if dreams die*
> *Life is a broken-winged bird*
> *That cannot fly.*
> *Hold fast to dreams*
> *For when dreams go*
> *Life is a barren field*
> *Frozen with snow.*

" 'A broken-winged bird' . . . I like that," he said softly.

I waited for him to go on. When he didn't, I kept talking, trying to fill the silent air around us.

"I guess, if you don't hang on to your dreams and take some risks, they can't help you get where you want to go. They just sort of die."

I didn't tell him why I liked the poem so much, how the first time I heard it a kind of movie started flashing through my mind. Every time I repeated Langston Hughes's words, I replayed the scene of my dad coming home. I could see Mom, looking up so surprised, then running over to make sure it was really him. The setting for the dream had changed since we moved to town. Now, instead of running across the sand to get to him, I jumped down the stairs into the lobby. But he still grabbed me and swung me around, laughing out loud. And then all three of us came together in a giant hug, and the scene faded out.

Lettie's father was looking at me. " 'A broken-winged bird.' "

"I still have the paper . . . with the poem on it, if you want to read it yourself."

He smiled. "I'd like that."

He gave my shoulder a squeeze. "Thanks for the talk, Mr. Slim. You really helped me."

He disappeared quietly into the kitchen. I guess I wasn't the only one trying to decide what to do. I wondered if my father had ever worried about doing the right thing for Mom and me. I tried to see him in my mind but the whole idea of my dad was shadowy, like he was more of a feeling than a person.

He hadn't been home much. And when he was home, it felt like Mom took care of him more than he took care of us. Of course, Lettie and Mrs. Mendoza, even Rosie, were always doing things for Mr. Mendoza too. Maybe I didn't have a good way to measure how much my father had worried about Mom and me or worked for us.

I thought about my crazy, little-kid dream, Dad coming home again. It wasn't going to happen. Did that mean my dream had died? Maybe it just changed. Maybe when I got old enough, I'd track Dad down. Not to drag him home, just to see him, to let him know everything turned out all right. I'd ask him why he left us, too, and tell him we got by okay without him. He probably wondered about that.

The noise of another truck rumbling down Main Street broke into my thoughts. I still had no idea how to approach

Calvin, Raymond, and the others. As the truck sounds faded, the quiet of the night pushed against the dim light coming from the windows. Taking a deep breath, I felt my mind starting to loosen up.

The kitchen door opened and Mom stepped out.

"Are you all right, *Shiyazh?*"

"Sure I am."

"What are you doing out here?"

"Thinking."

She shook her head. "Everyone is thinking tonight. Everyone is quiet, too quiet. I asked *'at'eed t'aa'athlaji yathtih'igii* why she's so quiet." I smiled at her description of Lettie, "the girl who always talks."

"She said, 'I'm just thinking.' When I asked her father what's wrong, he said the same thing. Everyone is strange tonight. Everyone is thinking."

My mother hugged herself and rubbed her arms. "I'm thinking that all this *thinking* may not be such a good thing."

She looked over at me expectantly. I shrugged. "But, since no one will tell me anything, I'm going to bed."

She went to the door. "Don't stay out here much longer, *Shiyazhi,* you need to get to sleep. You have school tomorrow."

A feeling of dread sped through me. Come on! I said to myself as the door closed. Get thinking! What are you going to do? I paced across the porch and back for a few minutes. Nothing! Then, softly, the sound of footsteps came around the corner of the hotel from the alley. The hair on my neck stood up for a few seconds as I waited for whoever was coming to move into the dim light from the kitchen.

It was Lorenzo. "*Yai!* You scared me!" he said when

127

he noticed me standing there. "I was just going to peek in the window and see if I could see you."

He walked up the steps and across the porch to me. "Are you all right?"

"I'm okay."

"Have you thought about school tomorrow . . . what it's going to be like?"

"I haven't thought about anything else all night."

"What are we going to do?"

"*We?*"

"Sure, we're friends, aren't we? We'll work this out together."

"I'm glad we're friends, *sik'is,*" I said, "but this is my problem. I'm going to have to solve it."

"Then what are *you* going to do?" He leaned on the railing like Mr. Mendoza had done.

"I don't know yet. That's why I came out here, to think about it." I walked over and sat on the top step, and he followed.

"I could walk right up and start swinging at Calvin's dopey face . . . but that wouldn't make sense. Maybe I could tease him until we got into a real fight. That sounds like a dumb thing to do too. It'd be stupid to start a fight to make up for a fight that I didn't finish in the first place."

Lorenzo got a puzzled expression. In a second, he nodded, but I wasn't sure he understood what I said.

"What I really want to do . . ."

He looked over.

". . . is develop a serious illness tonight . . . something that will keep me out of school for the rest of my life."

He laughed.

"I'd better get back home. I was taking the garbage out and decided to slip over here and check on you. My mother will think I'm out getting my nose broken again."

128

"Thanks for coming, *sik'is*."

"Remember, I'll be there with you tomorrow."

I nodded and he slipped into the darkness.

I walked back to my original thinking place and sat on the railing. Shoot! I still had no ideas!

The kitchen door opened and Lettie walked out.

"Are we still friends, Hobart?"

"We're friends," I said.

"What are you going to do?"

"I wish everybody would quit asking me that." I sighed. "I wish I'd quit asking myself."

Lettie paced up and down the porch. "Maybe it's something that you really can't plan. Maybe you have to see what happens and do what comes naturally."

I jumped down from the railing. "Lettie, you're a genius!"

"I am?"

"What a relief!"

"It is?"

"It's just like you said. There's no way to plan what to do tomorrow because I don't know what's going to happen. I've been dreaming up all kinds of things that Calvin might do or that I might do. But actually, there's no script. Everybody's going to have to ad lib. You can't really rehearse that kind of scene, you just react. It's the most challenging role I've ever had."

Lettie had stopped pacing. She stared at me as though I was crazy.

"I'm going to bed," I said. "I need all the rest I can get for tomorrow's performance."

I went in, glad to have the worrying behind me, and Lettie followed.

On the way upstairs, I remembered I'd promised to

share the poem with Mr. Mendoza. I found it and took it down to him.

He was sitting in the lobby, staring at the faded drapes. When I handed the paper to him, he said, *"Gracias,"* and started reading.

He must have read it a dozen times while I stood there.

"Keep it, if you want," I finally said. "Maybe you'll want to memorize it."

"I think I'll do that." He smiled again.

"It's a pretty good poem." I turned and started toward the stairs. "I got ten points for memorizing it."

I heard him chuckle as I went upstairs.

After getting ready for bed, I slid between my sheets. For a few minutes, I thought that I wasn't going to be able to turn off all the imaginary scenes jumping through my mind. But gradually, as I made my body relax, the action in my mind got slower and the images got dimmer, and finally the film just stopped rolling.

Chapter Fourteen

As soon as I woke up, all the things that happened the day before oozed over me like a gigantic blob of cold, sticky mud. Calvin and the tree house, Lettie, the bike, the fight ... everything whirled into my head like a scary movie.

I lay in bed examining my head, my throat, my stomach, anything that could possibly be sick. Nothing was. I counted to ten, got up, and went to take a shower.

In the middle of drying my hair, I looked into the steamy mirror and flexed my muscles. "If Calvin wants to fight today," I said softly to my hazy reflection, "I might just have to use my bicuspids instead of my biceps." It was a pretty funny joke, but my laugh came out in a sputtery little snort, hardly he-man quality.

After I got dressed, I looked up some perfect dictionary words to use on Calvin, just in case I got the chance. Then I went back to the bathroom mirror, to practice facing Calvin in front of all the kids at school.

I tried my regular friendly, joking approach. *Calvin, long time no see!* It didn't work.

How about a fierce, TV wrestler greeting? *Enjoy your morning, sleaze master, later today the scum of the earth gets washed down the drain!* My voice would probably crack, or I'd laugh and ruin the effect.

I finally settled on cool and serious. No greeting, just a calm stare to let Calvin know he mattered less to me than a fly would have mattered to Tyrannosaurus rex. It might work . . . if I remembered not to smile or wipe my sweaty palms on my pants.

Mom cooked breakfast, as usual. It was good . . . I think. She kept looking over and I didn't want her to ask a bunch of questions, so I tried my speedy eating system even though I didn't feel hungry. Lettie wasn't exactly enjoying breakfast either. I watched her drag a forkful of pancakes through the syrup on her plate. She lifted the fork toward her mouth, then put it back down without eating.

"Don't worry, Lettie," I said when Mom went to see if anyone else was ready to eat. "Everything will be fine."

"Thanks."

"Calvin and the other jerks will probably stay clear of you"—I winked—"and your powerful fists."

She didn't laugh.

"Oh, that," she said. "Actually, I was thinking about the Student Council meeting. It's the first one I've ever been to, you know."

"I forgot," I said. "Don't worry, that will turn out good too."

She nodded.

Before Mom got back, we scraped our plates into the trash can under the sink and went to brush our teeth. Then we left for school.

Just like I figured, there was already a crowd by the big tree. With my mind on automatic pilot, I kept walking. Last night, playing the scene without a script had sounded like a great plan. In the bright morning sunshine, it didn't seem like any plan at all. Just keep moving, I told myself. Stay loose and you'll be ready for anything.

I practiced my cool and serious look once more. In my mind, I looked like Clint Eastwood. What if I looked like a dope to everyone else?

As we moved closer to the tree, I could see Calvin and his friends. They weren't pushing each other around and laughing like they usually did. Was that good or bad? As they looked up and noticed Lettie and me, a miracle happened. Moving away from the tree, they went around toward the playground behind the school!

"Where are those guys going?" Lettie asked.

I shrugged.

"Did Calvin's cheek look a little swollen to you?"

I shrugged again. I'd been practicing my cool glance on the ground and hadn't looked directly at Calvin. So much for Clint Eastwood.

Lettie went over to talk to the girls and I looked for Lorenzo. He was sitting on the front steps.

"Did those guys say anything?" I slumped down beside him.

"Nothing. They acted like the great Lettie attack never even happened. As a matter of fact, they hardly said a word."

"I wonder why."

Lorenzo looked over at me. "Think about it, *sik'is*. If you'd been knocked down by a girl, would you want the world to know?"

He was right. Calvin was embarrassed, just like me!

"Do you think he'll just let it pass?"

Lorenzo shook his head. "I bet he's still mad. Calvin doesn't forget things."

I nodded.

"But look at the bright side," Lorenzo went on. "If Calvin beats you up, he won't do it in front of the whole school."

When he laughed I tried to join in, but my mouth felt too dry.

We were writing a Halloween story when Mrs. Buckley called Lettie to her desk to give her last-minute instructions about the Student Council meeting. Luckily, the pencil sharpener was right by Mrs. Buckley's desk and I had a pencil that took a long time to sharpen.

"Write down the key words, Lettie. Just enough so you can remember what Mr. Thomas and the others talk about. Then use your notes to report to the class."

Lettie clapped her hands to either side of her face just like a girl. I'd never seen her so nervous.

"You'll do fine. This is just an introduction meeting. I'll keep this list of ideas you gave me handy." Mrs. Buckley held up a piece of paper, then slipped it into her desk drawer. "Suggestions for school improvement will be discussed in later meetings."

What a relief! No playground cleanup during recess! No Hobart Slim, right-hand man and cleanup foreman! At least not for a while.

As Lettie went out the door, I flashed her a thumbs-up for good luck. She answered with a nervous smile.

Since the Student Council meeting lasted through recess, Lorenzo and I went to the jungle gym to hang around.

"Oh, oh," Lorenzo said and pointed with his lips. "Here comes trouble."

Calvin and the renegades were walking slowly across the blacktop toward us.

As they reached the jungle gym, Calvin crouched down, covering his head with his hands. "Watch out, men, it's that tough Hobart Slim."

He stood up and laughed. "Oh, I forgot. He's only tough when his *bodyguard* is around."

I'd been glancing from face to face with my meanest Clint Eastwood expression. No one seemed to notice. It was time for a new role.

"Calvin, you're the best!" I said cheerfully. "It must be your *simian* good looks that make you so popular."

The familiar puzzled look slipped onto his face.

"No, it's more than appearance. It's got to be your *hircine* qualities that lead all the best kids in town to *execrate* you."

Leo and the others were as puzzled as he was.

"I'm not sure what you're saying," Calvin said, "but I'll bet it's not good."

"Of course it's good. Even more important, it's all true."

A scowl scrunched his eyebrows. "You know, I'm getting sick of your fancy words, Hobart. You've been throwing them at me since school started."

A tiny spark of anger flickered somewhere in the middle of my chest. "To tell the truth, my simian friend, I'm getting sick of your comments about me too."

"Why don't you do something about it?"

I stood on the highest bar, wondering if I could jump down on top of him, smashing him into the sand, or if he'd raise his fists at the last minute, letting my own jump supply the power to knock my head off.

"I just might have to do that."

I could see the whole scene. We'd both go down on the sand, then roll, punching and kicking, out onto the blacktop. Oh-oh, rewind. Maybe I'd miss him. After all, my timing hadn't been very good lately. Maybe I'd thud onto the sand and the whole bunch of them would take turns using me for a punching bag.

"Well, go ahead. I'm waiting." He put his hands on his hips.

"I just might have to do that." Very original, Hobart! I told myself.

The bell rang.

"That's what I thought," Calvin said, turning to walk back to the school building.

I turned to Lorenzo. "If he really wanted to fight, why did he leave?"

Lorenzo shrugged.

Of course, Calvin hadn't been getting any younger, standing there waiting for me to make my move.

Lettie's report from the Student Council meeting was scheduled for right after lunch. As we passed the big tree on our way back from the "Chantmen Hot," Calvin was waiting for us.

"So, Lettie Mendoza, big class president, are you ready to give your report?" His voice was as warm as snowman sweat, but Lettie stayed calm.

"I think so."

He snorted. "I bet you're not!"

He spit on the sidewalk, then sauntered toward the building. Lettie and I exchanged a puzzled glance.

As soon as everyone settled down, Mrs. Buckley said, "Your class president has the report from our first Student Council meeting. Bring your notes, dear, and come up to the front of the room."

As Lettie passed him, Raymond stood and followed her up the aisle. People started laughing.

"Mrs. Buckley," Raymond said, "I have something in my eye."

While Lettie stood nervously beside her, the teacher peered into his eye. "I can't see anything. Come over by the window."

They moved across the room.

"Did you scratch your eye, Raymond? I can't see anything in there."

"It really hurts." I'd never known him to act so helpless.

"Well, you're in luck. Since it's Friday, the school nurse is here. Would someone please help Raymond down to the nurse's room?"

Raymond clamped his hand over his eye. "You take me, Mrs. Buckley . . . please!"

The teacher hesitated.

"It really hurts! I'll feel better if you take me down there."

"Very well," Mrs. Buckley said. "Lettie, you go right ahead and start your report. I'll be back as soon as I can." She turned to the rest of us. "I expect you to give your class president the respect she deserves, just as though I were here in the room."

As the teacher led Raymond out of the room, I saw Calvin smile slyly to Leo.

Lettie cleared her throat. "At the meeting this morning, Mr. Thomas suggested—"

Calvin stood up so fast his chair slammed against the desk behind him. "That's enough!" He walked to the front of the room.

"We don't want to hear anymore!" With a fierce expression on his face, he glanced from one side of the room to the other and back again. "By some mistake, Lettie, you got elected class president. Everybody realizes it was a mistake now and no one wants to listen to you."

Lettie finally found her voice. "Sit down, Calvin, and quit trying to show off."

He slouched back against the teacher's desk. "Don't worry, you're still president. Mrs. Buckley would never let us have another election. You can go to all the council meetings and stuff. Just don't expect anyone in this room to listen to what you have to say ... or do what you want us to.''

Lettie looked out at the class. "Does everybody feel this way?"

All the kids looked at the floor, except Calvin's friends. They nodded.

"That's right."

"You're finally catching on."

"Who'd listen to a girl?"

Lorenzo jumped to his feet. "I can't believe this!"

Calvin stood up straight. "Sit down, Manygoats, or I might have to break your nose again!"

Lorenzo's hand moved up toward his nose. Then he made a fist and lowered it to his side. "Go ahead and try it!"

Calvin took a step forward and Lettie grabbed his shoulder. He pulled away. "Don't even think about it," he snarled. "Yesterday I was caught off-guard ... It won't happen again."

As he started down the aisle toward Lorenzo, all the kids at the front of the room left their seats and scurried toward the back.

I felt weird. It was like I was acting in a movie, but at the same time, I was watching the scene from far away. Even though my heart was pounding, I wasn't thinking about getting hurt or losing control of the situation or making a fool of myself or any of the other things that had kept me out of action before.

Lettie grabbed the hair at the back of Calvin's head and he stopped short. With a wince on his face, he let his arm swing back and slugged her hard in the stomach. She let go, sagging against Mrs. Buckley's desk.

Before I even had a plan, I jumped to my feet and

started toward Calvin. Just who did he think he was? Somehow I had let him get by with hitting Lorenzo, but for sure he wasn't getting by with slugging Lettie! As long as I was around, Calvin Benally wasn't getting by with pushing anyone around from now on!

One row of desks stood between us. In a single motion, I pushed a desk into the aisle in front of the bully, blocking his path, and grabbed the front of his shirt.

He raised his arms to knock my hands away but I held on. "Stay out of this, Hobart, you might get hurt. Your girlfriend's out of commission, you know!"

I pushed him back into the next row of desks, knocking one over with a loud clatter. He raised his arms again, but my grip was strong. A button flew up and hit my forehead. I let go with my right hand, made a fist, and swung at Calvin's angry red face. My fist slammed straight into his jaw. Clint Eastwood would have been proud! As his head flew to the side, his body followed, ripping his shirt out of my hand. He lost his balance, grabbed a desk for support, and continued down, pulling the desk over with another crash.

In a few seconds, Calvin pushed himself up to his knees but didn't stand. He sank back onto his behind and carefully explored his bleeding lip with his fingers. That was all! He didn't get madder. He didn't rise up in a rage and try to kill me or get his friends to kill me. He just sat there.

"What in the world is going on here?!" Mrs. Buckley stood in the doorway, her hands on her hips. "I leave you people for two minutes and this is what happens!"

She walked to the front of the room, exploring the scene with angry eyes. "Hobart, I'm surprised at you . . . and very disappointed. Calvin, we've talked about this kind of behavior before. Both of you will visit with Mr. Thomas after school today."

"But, Mrs. Buckley—" Lettie started.

"Not a single word! I'm going to turn my back for thirty seconds, and when I turn around, I want this room in proper order and all of you in your seats."

She turned to face the clock above the chalkboard.

Half a minute later, we were all in place, eyes staring at the tops of our desks. Lettie raised her hand but the teacher ignored her.

"I will not allow a single word or gesture from any of you to disrupt the rest of our schoolday. Take out your social studies books and read chapter four. Answer every single question at the end of each section in complete sentences. You can be sure there will be a test on the material Monday morning!"

She noticed Calvin carefully wiping blood from his chin with the torn collar of his shirt. "Calvin, you may go to the lavatory and wash your face. If you're not back in five minutes, I will be down there to escort you back. The rest of you get busy!"

I thought Calvin would be sending fierce stares in my direction and muttering threats the rest of the afternoon, but he kept his nose in the social studies book like everybody else.

When the bell rang to go home, Lettie said, "I'll wait for you, if you want."

I shook my head. "No, you go ahead and go home. I don't know how long Mr. Thomas is going to keep us. I hear he can get pretty long-winded."

Lorenzo grinned. "I think sitting through his stories about when he was a boy is the worst. Sometimes I wish he'd just whack someone and get it over with." He patted me on the back. "You did good, Hobart."

I shrugged.

140

"I'll walk Lettie home, in case the rest of Calvin's friends want to cause some trouble."

"They won't." I don't know how I knew it with such certainty, but I did.

"I'll see you at the 'Chantmen Hot' then," Lettie said.

I nodded and headed down the hall toward Mr. Thomas's office.

Chapter Fifteen

Calvin was already sitting across from Mrs. Begay. She looked up as I walked in. "Take a seat, Hobart. Mr. Thomas is on the phone right now."

Since there were only two chairs, I sat next to Calvin.

The principal's door was open so we couldn't help but hear him. He laughed and talked, then laughed some more. He wasn't in any hurry to visit with us, and I was glad for that. The longer he talked, the more stories he told, the louder he laughed, the better mood he might be in when he got to Calvin and me.

I had practiced my cool look for Calvin all the way down the hall but I didn't have to use it. He didn't even glance my way. Both of us seemed fascinated by the picture on the wall behind Mrs. Begay's desk. It was a painting of a cattle drive.

All of a sudden, I thought about Mr. Mendoza and felt really sorry for him. Here he was, stuck with a job he didn't like very much, all because he had a responsibility to his family. I decided I'd go out of my way to cheer him up every chance I got.

Finally, Mr. Thomas said goodbye and I heard him hang up the phone. We waited another four and a half minutes— I kept track on the office clock—before he came to the door and said, "Hobart? Calvin? Come in here now."

He pointed to the two chairs across the desk from him and we sat down. After a few seconds of loud squeaking as he got comfortable in his big leather chair, he looked over at us.

"What is the school rule regarding fighting?" he said in a loud voice. "Hobart?"

"Don't fight, but—"

Mr. Thomas's voice got louder. "What is the school rule in regard to fighting, Calvin?"

"Don't fight, but—"

"The school rule is," the principal was shouting now. "No fighting ... period!" As he slammed his fist on top of his desk, Mrs. Begay closed his door, staying outside. "There isn't a thing you can tell me that justifies breaking that rule."

All the time I'd spent that afternoon, rehearsing my explanation of the fight, had been wasted. The only consolation was that Calvin didn't get a chance to talk either. I'm sure he had a pretty good story made up.

Mr. Thomas's volume stayed up. "You both need plenty of time to think about how inappropriate your behavior was this afternoon in Mrs. Buckley's classroom. And I'm just the person to arrange that time!" He thumped his desk again, and I swallowed. Calvin should have been used to this, but he didn't look all that comfortable either.

"You boys will work for me one hour after school every day for the next two weeks. I'm sure I can find many worthwhile projects for you to complete, starting with cleaning up the playground."

From the corner of my eye, I saw Calvin glance at me, but I kept looking at Mr. Thomas.

"And while you work, I want you to think of ways to resolve a difference of opinion without hurting each other. There are hundreds of excellent alternatives to fighting."

I think his shouting had worn him out. He leaned back in his chair and looked at us. "When I was a boy, we ran races to solve our problems."

I couldn't see how being the fastest runner made your solution best but I decided not to bring that up. I was ready to get out of there and head for the sympathy I knew everyone would give me at home.

Mr. Thomas was in no hurry. He told us one story after another about people he'd known who refused to fight and became popular because of it, but he never told us what some of those "excellent alternatives" to fighting were. I couldn't see the point behind some of the stories, like the time he was fishing and let a fish go instead of taking it home.

I glanced over at Calvin. He looked as dazed as I felt. I decided Mr. Thomas's plan was to scare us to death first and then bore us so much that we'd never fight again because we didn't want to end up in his office for more stories.

Finally, he ran out of when-I-was-a-boy examples. He sat there and looked from Calvin to me and back to Calvin for a few minutes. Then he turned his volume up again. "I will not tolerate fighting! In the next two weeks, you will both find out that I mean business!"

He gave a final thump to his desk and then lowered his voice. "Calvin, do you have anything you'd like to say to Hobart."

I guess Calvin knew the routine pretty well. "Sorry," he said.

"Hobart, how about you? What would you like to say to Calvin?"

"I'm sorry I busted your lip."

Mr. Thomas stood up. "There now, doesn't that feel

better? You boys shake hands. You're going to be seeing a lot of each other.''

As our hands met, I looked into Calvin's face. He looked like he was almost ready to smile. For a second, I could picture what it might be like if we were friends. It wasn't a bad picture.

Walking down the hall next to Calvin, I said, ''Did you understand that fish story?'' I thought he'd laugh.

He just looked over at me and scowled. So much for being friends. We continued down the hall, side by side, without saying a word. When we got outside, he went his way and I went mine.

Turning the corner, I saw the Mendozas' station wagon parked in front of the ''Chantmen Hot.'' As I got closer, I noticed it was packed full and Lettie's bike had been tied on top. Just as I reached the steps, she burst out of the front door.

''Finally! What took you so long?''

''It was Mr.—''

''I was so afraid I wouldn't get the chance to say goodbye.''

''Goodbye?''

''But I stalled them. I kept telling Daddy that we had to see you before we left. Who knows when we'll come this way again, especially if things work out good at the Flying Deuce. But Daddy kept saying that we have to get going and I could just write you a letter from Wyoming and that would be better anyway because saying goodbye is sort of sad.''

I knew she wasn't going to run out of words very soon. Grabbing her shoulders, I pulled her down so we could sit on the steps side by side.

''What happened?'' I asked. ''When did you guys decide to go on to Wyoming? What about the Foodtown job?''

''When I got home from school, they had the car all loaded, except for my bike. It wouldn't fit. I used it as an excuse to stall for time too. I told Daddy that I *had* to take my bike, it was the best present I ever got in my whole life.''

''Lettie! You'd better cut it short.''

''Oh, right.'' She took a deep breath. ''My dad had everyone sitting in the lobby when I got home, even your mom and Uncle Tully. He told us that he knew we were happy about the job offer from Foodtown, but he really wanted to be a computer *cowboy*, not a computer *grocery-man*. He said he knew we liked it here, but how would we know that we didn't like Wyoming better if we didn't go there and try it out? He said that if we absolutely didn't want to give the Flying Deuce a try, he'd stay here and work it out the best way he could, but he would probably always wish we'd taken the risk and gone on to Wyoming.

''Then he read us some poem about squeezing your dreams so they didn't turn into dead birds. I didn't really get that part because I was trying not to feel so disappointed about leaving the 'Chantmen Hot' and the school and Lorenzo and . . . you.''

I didn't get the chance to respond to that because everybody came bustling out of the hotel and Mr. Mendoza started getting his family settled in the station wagon.

Lettie rolled down the window and I went over.

''What's your father's big hurry,'' I said. ''Couldn't you guys wait until tomorrow morning?''

Lettie shrugged.

''Maybe he's afraid you and your mom will change your minds.''

''I don't think that's it. He knows we think he's the

146

best man in the whole world. He can do anything . . . except fix cars." She laughed. "Maybe he's afraid that *he*'ll change his mind."

Mom and Mrs. Mendoza were saying goodbye. Lettie's dad stepped over and handed me a folded piece of paper. It was the poem.

"Thank you, *amigo,*" he said and laid his hand on my shoulder.

"Don't you want to keep it . . . in case you can't remember . . . ?"

He smiled. "I won't forget."

"Oh, Hobart, I'm such a dope," Lettie said, leaning out the car window. "Thanks for sticking up for me today. You were wonderful!"

I felt my face turning red and looked away. Mr. Mendoza was looking at Lettie with that loving, proud expression on his face. I noticed Mom listening to us. She was looking at me with the same expression.

"Bye, Hobart," Rosie said, and blew me a kiss.

"You take care of yourself, Rosie Mendozie."

"I'll write and send you our address," Lettie promised.

Mr. Mendoza got in and started the station wagon. In a cloud of blue smoke, they were on their way. We watched them drive down the street until they went around the bend. All of a sudden, I felt as empty as that street.

I looked down at the paper still clutched in my hand.

"What's that?" Mom asked.

"A poem." I handed it to her and she read it silently.

"I like that." She handed the paper back and went in.

When dreams go, I thought. Probably my dream of tracking down my dad would go, just like the one of him coming home and surprising us.

It doesn't matter, I told myself, and I believed it. Mom and me, and maybe Uncle Tully too, are a family. Just

147

like Lettie and her mom and dad and Rosie. No matter how many there are in your family, that's just the right number.

The weekend seemed as long and empty as Main Street had after the Mendozas drove away. Even Lorenzo couldn't fill it up. While we sat in the tree house, talking about Lettie and how different it was going to be without her, I found out I'd learned some things.

Thanks to Lettie, I'd stood up for myself. I wasn't going to sit back and wait for the world to change for me. First, I'd try to change it myself. If I couldn't, I'd change to fit into it. If I wanted something to happen, I'd better get busy and make it happen.

"I guess you'll be class president, now that Lettie's gone," Lorenzo said.

"I guess so." Somehow it didn't seem so important anymore.

I thought of the times I had wished she'd never come. Now I'd give anything to have her back here. Shoot! I'd even be her playground cleanup assistant. Then I remembered that Mr. Thomas had already given me that job.

The next week, school was different. For one thing, Calvin stopped hassling me. It might have been that he was too tired after all the work we had to do. Maybe it had something to do with spending an hour a day together. A couple of times I almost got him to laugh.

Some of the kids started inviting Lorenzo and me to play basketball with them. Instead of waiting for someone to ask me to be friends, I started scouting out kids to include in the game. Lorenzo was still my best friend, but he liked playing with the other kids as much as I did.

On the second Thursday after Lettie left, I was walking past the barn and noticed my old bike, still lying on the floor with the paint cans. If it was ever going to get fixed, it was up to me.

I dragged it around in front to the sidewalk where it's level. Lorenzo showed up and helped me take the wheel off so I could fix the tire.

"Do you know how to fix a flat tire?" he asked.

"Not really. How about you?"

"Nope, I've never even owned a bike." Something up the street caught his attention. "Why don't you ask your old friend, Calvin Benally?"

Sure enough, Calvin was riding his bike toward us.

"Why not?" I said, and grinned at his astonished look.

"Hey, Calvin!" He slowed down. "Do you know anything about fixing a flat tire?"

His eyes narrowed. "Of course I do. I know just about everything there is to know about bikes."

"How would you like to help us fix this thing?"

He rode on down the street a few yards, then circled back to coast in close to us. "I might, Hobart. I just might."

Glossary

NAVAJO WORDS

Before listing individual words with their meanings, let's look at a literal translation of three phrases used in the book. You might get a glimpse of the structure of the Navajo language.

'at'eed	t'aa'athlaji'	yathtih'igii
(the girl)	(all the time)	(the one who talks)

Or "the girl who talks all the time"

Notice that adjectives usually follow nouns in Navajo.

Haishii	yith	beehozin?
(Who)	(with him)	(there is knowledge)

Or "Who knows?"

Verbs generally come at the end of the sentence.

Kin	goné	yah iiya.
(The house)	(inside)	(he went)

Or "He went inside the house."

It's a fascinating language, isn't it?

at'ah—wait (a request, as in "wait here")

at'eed yazhi—little girl

bilagaana—white person

chidi—car

dilkooh—smooth

hagoshii—all right

ha'at'iish biniye?—why? (for what purpose)

shida'—my nephew

shida'i—my uncle

shima—my mother

shiyazh—my son (mother speaking)

shiyazhi—my little one

sik'is—my friend (of the same gender, male to male, female to female)

t'aa akoon dasoozi—wait right here

tsin 'ii'aii 'ati' doothliith—they will harm the tree

SPANISH WORDS

gracias—thank you

hombre—man

mi'jita—my daughter

si—yes

amigo—male friend

HOBART'S DICTIONARY WORDS

If you want exact definitions, you can look up the following words for yourself. These are Hobart's meanings for the words.

bicuspids (bī kus' pid)—the teeth at the front of your mouth that have two points on them

execrate (eks' i krāt)—to hate with all your heart

fetid (fet' id)—having a terrible odor, stinking

hircine (her' sīn)—smelling like a goat

miasma (mī az' ma)—the stinky gases that rise from things that are rotting

nystagmus (nis tag' mus)—twitching eyeballs

plebeian (pli bē' an)—common or low-class

plinth (plinth)—the slab of rock at the bottom of a column in fancy buildings

popinjay (pop' in jā)—a person who thinks he's more terrific than he really is

simian (sim' e an)—resembling an ape or monkey

suet (su' it)—hard animal fat

wivern (wī' vern)—a monster with two clawed feet, two wings, and a tail like a snake

wizened (wiz' nd)—withered or shriveled up